The Survivors

T. C. Weber

Published by Freedom Thorn Press, 2025.

This is a work of fiction. Similarities to real people, places, or events are entirely coincidental.

THE SURVIVORS

First edition. March 9, 2025.

ISBN: 978-1736901762

Written by T. C. Weber.

To all those fighting climate change before the effects
are catastrophic and irreversible.

Don't give up.

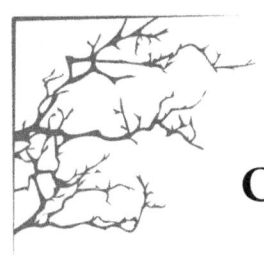

Chapter One

Low, dark clouds obscure the moon and stars as I step into one of our flat-bottomed wooden boats. A warm, salty breeze from the northeast whips the wide black waters, rocking the boat, but too feebly to capsize it. For now, anyway. A storm is coming.

Angelica calls to me from the floating walkway surrounding our seven-floor tower home. "It looks a little rough out there, Lucy."

"Boat's not taking on water," I tell her. "Just don't stand once we're away."

Angelica is young and attractive, with dark eyes, braided hair, and smooth, honey-colored skin. She is bulging with her first child and probably shouldn't be out here, but my aunt Irma says it's easy work and she'll be fine. Maybe Irma's right. I lost my first child, but I wasn't born in the tower like Angelica, with plenty to eat and no nearby enemies.

I reach out my arms and help my friend on board. She settles onto the back bench and eyes the clouds with worry on her face.

"We'll head back before the storm arrives," I say. We have plenty of time, especially if we stick close to the tower instead of foraging up side creeks, our usual task. Cattails and other plants have edible or medicinal parts, and supply fiber and

1

lining for clothes, mats, and baskets. One good thing about the breeze—it keeps away 'skeetos and biting flies, which gave me the shaking chills last year and killed Irma's newborn. When the bugs are bad, we have to daub mud or allium oil on our skin to keep them off.

"Where are the others?" Angelica asks.

"Rod and Griff are checking the fish traps." Irma's teenage sons are arrogant and a little frightening, but they're fast rowers. I point to the east. "Irma and Thal are over there." Their boat is about a hundred yards from the tower, barely visible in the dark. They've stopped rowing, and the boat rocks slightly in the waves. Thal stands up with his net, then stumbles. Irma grabs his arm and says something I can't make out—probably telling him not to be so clumsy. Thal turns and casts his net into the water.

"Let's stay close and catch crabs," I say.

Near the tower, the bottom is covered with tangled metal. Fish nets take days to make, and we can't afford to snag or rip one. On cloudless days, when the wind is calm, the blinding sun illuminates the shattered remains of buildings, fences, and wheeled machines beneath the surface. Closer to the marshy shore lies the remnants of a giant flying machine, its wings and tail broken off. Further offshore, where Irma and Thal are fishing, the bottom is flat, with wide roads that end abruptly.

We paddle a short distance from the tower, tie rank-smelling fish heads on our crab lines, and lower them into the water. I hold a finger against my line and wait to feel the vibration of a feeding crab. We haven't crabbed this spot for a while, so I hope we'll get lucky.

"Puya!" Angelica squeals behind me. She speaks my language as well as I do, but knows her ancestors' also.

I turn my head toward her. "Got one already?"

"No, it's my baby. I feel it kicking and punching, like it wants to get out."

It's better off staying inside, I think. But I don't tell Angelica this.

"I think it's a muchacho," she says, "the way it kicks so hard."

"Girls kick hard too." Mary, my oldest child, certainly did, although she's been a darling since she emerged.

I suspect Irma was especially ferocious in the womb. Thal has never hit me, but Aunt Irma has beaten me a dozen times since we fled our birth territory. Irma is bigger and more savage than me, and doesn't stop until her opponent is on the ground or dead. My free hand touches the ragged stump of my left ear, a gift from Irma the last time we fought.

Angelica fingers the totem around her neck, a metal cross from the ancient times. "Ángeles del Mundo Desaparecido, Spirits of the Vanished World, please give us lots of crabs today."

Her birth group, she'd told me, prayed to the Vanished Ones every day. It didn't help them. "If there are spirits here," I say, "they don't respond."

Angelica frowns at me. "That's not true. They're giving me a healthy baby. And they gave me Thal."

"Thal's attention drifts with the winds," I say.

Angelica sniffs at me. "Thal saved me from Irma's blade. He adores me and makes me happy."

"When Irma and I captured Thal," I say, "I was only nine and he focused his attentions on Irma. But once I was old enough, he lay mostly with me. Like you, I thought he loved me more than Irma. But love is beyond him. He just likes sex and you're newer." And once Angelica began bulging, I don't add, Thal turned his attention back to me and Irma.

Angelica pouts. "You're the new ones, chera. My group was here before any of you were born."

I hate arguing with my only friend—'chera' in her people's language. Angelica hasn't lost all her anger, though. Maybe remnants will always cling deep inside.

Most of her group had died from the pox before we arrived. We were desperate and Irma had plotted to take the tower and its waters by ambushing their remaining adults while they foraged. I'd argued that we should merge with their group instead, and work together. Irma had insisted the world didn't work that way, and everyone else had agreed.

"I'm sorry about what happened," I tell Angelica. Fourteen at the time, she'd begged for her life and Thal had happily granted it. "But we're all family now," I continue. "I love you like I love my children."

"I love you too." She twirls her salt-scented braids, one of those cute things she does when she's happy. She's the only one in our group with long hair, and needs my help to periodically wash and braid it. In return, she tattooed Vanished World flying machines on my arms—a painful process, but permanent reminders that it's possible to build such things.

I feel a faint tug on my line. "Net," I tell Angelica.

She pulls up her line and grabs the hand net.

I bring my line in slowly. Too quick, and fear will overcome the crab's hunger. The bait breaks the surface. An adult blue crab grips the fish head, still stuffing pieces into its mouth.

Angelica thrusts the hand net beneath and we have our first crab. Judging by the narrow hinge on its belly, a male. We need a lot more for a filling meal, but something is always better than nothing.

Angelica rubs her totem. "Muchas gracias, Espíritus."

I wonder why the people of the Vanished World created totems. They were like gods themselves. They built the tower and millions of other things. They had wheeled machines—their remains are everywhere—that sped down the roads. According to stories passed down in my birth village, their flying machines crisscrossed the sky, taking people wherever they wanted to go. My one dream is to recover enough of their ancient knowledge to make life easier for my children.

The sun should be glowing on the eastern horizon by now. But it's still dark. "Have you seen a storm come from the east?" I ask Angelica. Normally, they come from the west.

"Almost never. But when it happens, they're bad."

I paddle the boat a little closer to the tower but we can't go in yet. It hasn't started raining and we only have one crab.

WE CATCH FIVE MORE crabs worth keeping, then the wind picks up and it starts to rain. Dark clouds obscure the east. Time to go in, whether Irma likes it or not.

I paddle back to the tower and tie the boat to the big metal hooks Angelica's group had pounded into the wall. I push open the hand-carved wooden door covering the old window frame—we'd left it unlatched—and climb inside with the bucket of crabs.

Torches cut from hardwood saplings rest in metal stands around the concrete room. The upper ends have been split four ways, with resin-soaked balls of bark fiber stuffed in between. I grab a flint and steel from one of the supply shelves against the furthest wall, and hold the flint against one of the torch ends. I strike the steel against the flint edge, throwing sparks against the fuel. After about ten times—I'm not the best at this—it finally lights. I place the lit torch against two others—we'll need at least three.

Irma and Thal enter. Thal carries a basket of fish. He's tall and strong, with a short beard he trims once a month with a knife. He wears a "luck-bringing" necklace made from crow feathers, mouse skulls, and fish bones. Irma, our leader, is in her mid-thirties, sturdy, and shaves her head to keep lice off. She wears see-far glasses around her neck, two joined black tubes with glass ends that make distant objects seem close—an incredibly useful Vanished World tool we found in the top floor of the tower.

Rod and Griff are still out there. Irma returns to the doorway and looks through her see-far glasses. She lowers them and barks, "Hurry, you dirt-brains!"

The rain and wind have grown stronger by the time Irma's sons arrive with more fish from the traps. Rod is adult-sized, but with only wisps of facial hair. Griff is almost Rod's height, but still growing.

"Big catch," Griff says.

Irma slaps the side of his head, then does the same to Rod. "You should have come in earlier."

Rod glares at her. "We had to finish checking the traps."

Irma slaps him again. "What good is that if you drown in a storm? Now go clean those fish."

It's a bad idea to be around Irma when her temper's aflame. I take one of the torches and lead Angelica up the zig-zagging concrete stairs. The children aren't in the sleeping rooms, so they must have gone up to the top, where we cook and eat.

We climb another set of stairs and emerge onto the top floor, high above the water. It's a little smaller than the lower floors, a five-pointed room ringed with big glass windows that slant outward. Below the circle of windows, at waist height, runs a thick shelf with old machines angled up against the bottom edge of the glass. None of them work, but it's fun guessing what they were for. The black rectangles with rows of letters and numbers must have been for writing. And the half-disintegrated headpieces might have been used for speaking to people outside the room.

From the windows, you can see practically the whole estuario—Angelica's word for the wide river mouth—although not all the way to the ocean. The ground is mostly flat, with some low hills to the west. Because of the slant, rain almost never hits the windows, but this time the wind is dashing it against the panes facing the storm.

My four-year-old daughter, Mary, sees me. She's holding Isaac, still short of his first year.

"Mama!" Mary shouts, a big smile on her face.

I give the crabs to Irma's daughters—Bree, who's ten, and Tash, who's seven. They do most of the cooking. A long-gone former resident had placed an iron stove against one window and fed a pipe through the ceiling to get rid of the smoke. Irma's daughters have already lugged pails of brackish water up the stairs and started a fire inside the stove. Bree fills a pot with water and dumps in the wriggling crabs, along with the rest of the plant leaves we'd gathered yesterday.

I lift Mary and Isaac up in the air. They squeal in delight.

"You are such a joy, you two!"

"I love you, Mama!" Mary says. She's such a darling.

I put Mary down, sit in a tattered plastic chair with wheels on the bottom, and breast-feed Isaac.

Thal, Rod, and Griff bring up the fish fillets, give some to Bree to fry on the stove, and start salting the rest to preserve them. We eat the crabs, fish, and greens as soon as they're cooked, sitting on woven floor mats in a big circle. Tash passes out hardtack squares made from ground roots, seeds, and evaporated salt. They have to be soaked in bowls of warm water or they're impossible to chew.

Mary smashes a crab claw with her grinding stone and a shell fragment flies out of the bowl and hits me in the cheek. Her eyes widen. "Oops."

I laugh so she won't worry. "Don't hit it so hard."

Next to us, Thal laughs too and rubs her head. "You'll make a good warrior someday."

She grins at him. "I want to be smart like mama!"

I cringe, but Thal just laughs again.

Outside, the wind grows stronger, driving the rain horizontally. Air screeches between the window panes. Isaac starts to cry and I have to hold him. "Don't worry, this is the safest place in the world."

Our tower has stood since before the fall of the Vanished World. Even the glass is intact. It's the most defensible home we've ever had, and it's surrounded by food and water.

Angelica scoots close to me. She looks scared. "I never saw wind like this."

"We'll be alright." I fetch the small pile of ancient books from beneath the window counter. "Shall we read?"

She grins. "Yes."

According to Angelica, the books had been in the tower since before she was born, possibly brought by whoever installed the stove. No one in her group had ever bothered with them. The original binding glue had disintegrated, but I'd made new glue by mixing pine sap, charcoal powder, ground bark, and a little muskrat fat. Thal had laughed at my efforts, saying I could just tie the pages together, but I'd told him the closer we follow the ways of the Vanished Ones, the better off we'll be.

Between the guide books and picture books written for young children, I've taught myself a lot of words, although the only ones I'm sure how to pronounce are from *The Word Book* and *First 200 Words*, like "tree" and "dog."

I open the plant guide. I show Mary the pages showing different kinds of leaves and flowers. "If you learn to identify plants and mushrooms, you'll know which ones are useful and which are bad."

In the plant guide, I've used a charcoal stick to circle the edible plants and draw X's next to the poisonous ones. I flip to white snakeroot, which has an X next to the picture. "This could kill you. It has opposite toothed leaves and clusters of small white flowers on top."

Mary is only four—although nearly five—but she's much smarter than any of Irma's children when they were her age. She learns quickly, and remembers what I tell her.

I point to some of the words I've figured out. "Lower leaves stalked." I've taught the alphabet to everyone but Thal, who considers it a waste of time. Irma admits the guide books are useful, but most of the others—the ones with only words—she gave to her daughters to light the stove with. As soon as Isaac's weaned, I hope to search the shore for more books, especially ones that can teach how to read. We can learn what's been forgotten, pass down the knowledge, and make our lives easier and more pleasant. Assuming the books haven't all disintegrated or been used to start fires.

Mary loses interest in the plant guide. "Let's try fixing the machines again."

"They need power," I say, "and we don't have any."

She turns to Angelica. "Can you call the Vanished Ones to come fix the machines?"

Angelica pats her shoulder. "I've tried. They don't always listen."

Not for the first time, I wonder if Vanished Ones still exist far away, and if they might return someday and fix the broken world.

The tower begins to creak and groan. Everyone looks up, fear on their faces. The sky is black and furious, rain hammering against the glass. My muscles clench with every new noise.

"Look!" Bree shouts. She points out the southeast windows.

Everyone crowds to the window. A churning wall of water speeds toward us, many times higher than any waves I've seen before. Knees shaking, I grip my daughter and infant and back away.

Angelica grips her talisman and challenges the approaching waves. "Por favor, deténganse, Espíritus! Los adoraremos mejor!"

The tower shudders and shakes. Spray slaps up the windows, like the water's trying to pull us down.

The window in front of Angelica cracks, jagged lines marching across its surface. It shatters inward. Shards of glass fly into the room, along with howling wind and spray strong enough to knock everyone off their feet—even Thal. Lengths of grass tear away from my woven vest and skirt.

Angelica screams, a high-pitched shriek that sounds like an animal being ripped apart.

I try to get up, but the wind is too strong. More windows break. Pieces of the ceiling fall.

"Downstairs!" Irma shouts. Everyone scrambles for the stairs.

Mary and Isaac are my main concern. I crawl along the floor with them and shout to Thal, "Help Angelica!"

The stairs are slick with rainwater. I carry Isaac in one arm and grip the metal railing with the other. Mary follows, holding my waist and whimpering.

As we enter our sleeping room, Thal arrives, half-carrying Angelica. Bright red blood streams from her left eye. A shard of glass is lodged in her pupil, protruding out almost an inch. She gasps and wails, arms flailing.

Thal lays Angelica on her bed mat of woven grass and feather down. This is her sleeping room too. Blood oozes down her cheek. Thal reaches a hand toward her eye. "Stay still."

Angelica is anything but still, head and arms shaking as she cries out. Thal's hand stops short of the glass like he's not sure what to do.

"Hold her head still," I say. He grips her temples with his big hands. Irma comes in and holds her body down.

"Anyone else hurt?" I ask Irma.

"Some cuts and bruises," she says. "Nothing serious."

Thal looks at me. "You can get the glass out?"

I'm not sure. I reach a thumb and forefinger toward the glass shard. Angelica's eyebrows climb her forehead, and her good eye widens in terror. "Por favor, ayúdame." *Help me.*

I grip the end of the shard, trying not to slice my fingertips. Slowly, I pull it out of her eye. Angelica moans and wails but Thal and Irma keep her from thrashing. I feel like vomiting but keep pulling.

The glass emerges from her eye with a sucking sound. Blood and clear fluid ooze out.

I press Angelica's hand over the wound. "Hold it there till I return."

I rummage through the medicine pack and pull out two plantain leaves. My mother was the clan healer when I was a child—the most important job there is—and taught me everything she knew. Plantain brings down inflammation and helps prevent 'fection, and makes a good bandage.

I wash the leaves thoroughly, then crush one and make a poultice. Taking care to avoid the puncture, I place the poultice onto her eye and secure the second leaf on top with twine around her head. "You have to lie on your back for a while."

To reduce the pain, I give Angelica a sliver of willow bark. "Chew this." Then I hold her hand and try to comfort her.

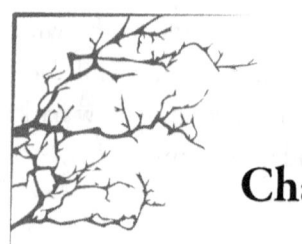

Chapter Two

Hours later, the howling wind stops. I enter the wet stairwell with Thal and Irma to assess the damage. The bottom level, where we store our fishing gear and access the boats, is underwater. The top floor is wrecked. All the windows are gone and half the roof has collapsed.

The sky is clear and sunny. But the marshes are completely submerged, and there's no sign of the fish traps. I hope the boats are alright, but we can't see them from this angle.

We try to salvage what we can from the top. The stove is the most valuable thing, but it's too heavy to move.

"How'd they get this up here?" I ask.

Irma shrugs. "We can fix the roof. Not the windows, but we don't need them."

The books—the ones up here anyway—are soaking wet, but maybe I can dry them. As we shuttle cooking gear, salted fish fillets, and books downstairs, the wind and rain return—this time from the opposite direction.

"It's not done with us," Thal says. "It wants us dead."

Irma scowls at the returning storm and casts an ancient curse: a raised middle finger and the words, "Go fuck yourself."

We huddle below as the storm smashes against the tower again. What else can we do? If we leave in the boats, we'll capsize and drown.

Moaning a little, Angelica rubs her talisman as she lies in bed. I need regular food to produce milk for Isaac, and rummage through my survival pouch for the fire-making tools. This pouch kept me alive nine years while wandering with my aunt Irma, my cousins, and Thal, but now I almost never use it.

I sacrifice part of the rush mat between the beds in our sleeping room and weave the stalks together so they'll take longer to burn. I arrange the kindling into a tepee in the concrete stairwell. The floor is damp, but the stairs above will shelter the fire while allowing the smoke to escape. Inside the tepee, I place some feathers and cattail down from my bed.

Thal joins us. "We must be strong. At least we're all alive."

"If you want to help me," I say, "you can bring some dry wood and the old cooker."

He orders Irma's children to do it. Bree brings wood from the storage room. Tash brings the disassembled cooking platform we'd designed before discovering the tower. They stack some of the wood around the kindling and set the rest to the side. I assemble the metal rods of the cooker, forming a frame around the wood, and fasten the pan just above where the flames will be.

I prefer Thal's method for starting fires, a stick and bow. My parents used this method too. I press my drill stick against a narrow hole in a base board and spin the stick with a bow and thong. The grinding creates red-hot dust, which drops onto a large metal spoon filled with shavings of pine pitch mixed with cattail down. The spoon's handle lies inside a wood casing I carved, so my fingers won't burn. I blow gently on the tinder and ignite it, then dump it inside the kindling tepee. It catches fire immediately.

I tend to overcook things, so I let Bree cook the fish. We eat it with more hardtack, already damp from the rain.

Afterward, I sing to my children, picking one of the ancient tunes my mother used to sing when I was a child. Irma and I don't believe in spirits, but a good song can mean whatever you want.

> *Amazing grace, how sweet the sound,*
> *That saved a wretch like me*
> *I once was lost, but now am found,*
> *Was blind, but now I see*
> *Through many dangers, toils and snares,*
> *I have already come*
> *'Tis grace that brought me safe thus far,*
> *And grace will lead me home*

The water in the stairwell continues to rise. I worry that it will submerge the entire tower and drown us.

Finally, the storm fades away. I return upstairs with Thal and Irma.

The whole roof is gone and everything smashed, including the stove. Broken glass crunches beneath our thick moccasins. The land is flooded as far as I can see. Only the hills to the west peek above the water. Most of the visible pine trees have been snapped in half.

Irma scans the horizon with her see-far glasses and grinds her teeth.

My heart thumps in panic. The room with our fishing gear is underwater and the marshes are gone. We only have two or three days of food in the tower. What about the boats? Can we row to the hills to search for food?

I climb over debris and out one of the broken windows, cutting my leg in the process. There's a lower roof just below—the rest of the tower is wider than the top section. I lean over the side where we moor two of our four boats.

They're gone. Even the walkway is gone.

I rush to the other side.

They're gone too.

I TELL IRMA AND THAL the bad news.

"Are you sure?" Irma asks. "All four boats?"

"Yes."

She explodes into red-faced rage, snarling and screaming. I cringe as she hurls broken Vanished World machines at the sky. They splash into the water below.

Then she stomps back down the stairs. I follow at a safe distance.

She asks Angelica, who is still lying in bed, "Can you show us how to build more boats?"

Angelica stiffens and she props herself up on her elbows. Pinkish liquid seeps from beneath her eye bandage. "What happened to the boats?"

"The storm took them," I say. "It destroyed the top of the tower too."

Angelica collapses back on the bed. Tears emerge from her good eye. "Can we fix it?"

"Do you know how the boats were built?" Irma repeats.

"They were made before I was born."

Irma's eyebrows knot in anger. "You don't know how?"

Angelica's face returns the anger. "Pinche pendeja! You shouldn't have killed Sam, Mia, and Felipe. Felipe knew how to fix the boats and I'm sure he could build a new one. Why'd you have to kill them, puta?"

I feel guilty for my part in their death. They didn't even have a chance to resist. Irma had spied on them and learned their routines, and waited for them to gather plants and check their fish traps, when they'd be close to shore. Irma, her sons, and Thal hid in the reeds and shot arrows into all three.

I didn't shoot anyone—I'd been watching Mary, then an infant, and Irma's young daughters. And before the ambush, I'd suggested an alliance. When no one agreed, I argued that at least we could capture them alive and exile them. Thal had been exiled from his birth group after he challenged his leader and lost. They didn't kill him. But Irma always expected the worst from others, and insisted that Angelica's group would stay nearby and find a way to kill us. I could have warned Angelica's group, forced a compromise. But instead, I'd given in.

Irma never bothered to learn Español, but curses are obvious no matter the language. She leans toward Angelica's face. "Tell me what 'puta' means, if you dare."

Her anger will turn to rage if I don't do something. "Angelica needs to rest," I say. "I have to change her bandage now."

"She's useless." Irma stomps out.

I wash my hands and remove Angelica's eye patch. The underside of the plantain leaf glistens with blood-soaked jelly. Her eyelids are dark red and shut.

"Can you open your eye?" I ask.

Her left eye is bright red. The pupil is a thin, ragged oval instead of a circle. "All I see is red in that eye," she says.

I clean the wound and put on a new leaf, tighter than before. I hope her body can repair itself. Otherwise, we'll have to remove the eye.

AFTER A DAY, THE WATER level has receded some, but the floor with our fishing nets is still submerged. Thal volunteers to retrieve them but Irma says it will be dark and they can't risk him drowning over a few nets. We remove the boards covering the small windows in the sleeping section, search through the top floor wreckage, and make fishing lines, hooks, and sinkers from wires and pieces of metal.

We spend all day and night fishing out the windows, but don't even get a nibble. The storm must have been even harder on the fish and crabs than it was on us.

Irma puts everyone on half rations except me—I'm breast feeding—and Angelica—who's pregnant and injured. Thal says he should get full rations too, and then everyone argues.

"If I'm on half rations," Irma tells Thal, "so are you."

"Why?"

"Because you eat so much."

WE RUN OUT OF SALTED fish and hardtack, and still haven't caught anything. Not even the wading birds have returned. We make new nets from the floor matting, but have no success with those either. The waters have dropped by half, but are still not back to normal.

Irma calls a meeting. We sit on woven mats in the big room she shares with her children and Thal. "We must swim to shore," she says, "and leave this place."

"This place is cursed," Thal says.

"In a way it's a blessing," Irma says. "We need to find mates for Rod and Griff."

"Thal shouldn't have got Angelica," Rod says. "He already had Lucy."

I ready myself for the argument to come, but Thal leaps to his feet and curls his big hands into fists. "You were a child then and you're a child now."

"Everyone shut up," Irma says. "Yesterday was yesterday, today is today. We must build rafts for our supplies."

"And my children?" I ask. "They're too young to swim. And Angelica can't swim in her condition."

"We'll build them rafts too."

I nod. It's a reasonable plan. "When we get to shore, we can stay close. Maybe where we camped before taking the tower." I feel guilty every time I think about that. "The waters will recede eventually, and the marsh plants should grow back."

"We'll see," Irma says.

Not exactly the answer I wanted, but the future's still open. And Irma usually acts in the group's interest, and is right more often than wrong.

We unscrew wooden doors from their hinges and lash our bedding on top to keep our deerskins dry. Plus one guidebook—Irma won't let me bring more. Our rafts look clumsy, and would make terrible fishing boats, but if the loads aren't too heavy, they shouldn't sink.

When the eastern horizon begins to glow, we load our belongings—whatever we can carry later—onto two rafts, and slide them into the water. Irma's sons and daughters jump in and guide the rafts toward the distant shore, pushing floating branches and uprooted plants out of the way.

I ease into the water with them. I'm not a great swimmer like Rod and Griff, but think I can make it to shore now that the water's still again. I coax Mary onto a third raft and place Isaac in her arms. The top of the door drops below the surface, but barely—my children are light.

"Mary," I say, "hold Isaac as if his life was your own."

She looks frightened, but does as I ask.

Angelica is heavier than the other loads. We've built a special raft for her—two doors with firewood fastened between. It keeps her afloat as Thal and Irma swim with it.

My legs don't reach bottom, but I hold my children's raft with one hand and kick with my feet. We move slowly and the shore doesn't seem to get much closer. A log bumps against the raft and spins us around.

Thal and Irma have no trouble with Angelica's raft. It isn't fair—they're both much stronger than me. Angelica is vulnerable, but what about my baby, who can't swim at all?

I'm not getting anywhere. The current is too strong and I can't keep the raft from drifting downstream. Everyone else makes it to shore, but I run out of energy.

I start to panic. "Help!"

The others unload their rafts—either they can't hear me or they don't care. Isaac and Mary start to cry.

"Please help!" I lose my grip on the raft. My head slips beneath the murky surface and I swallow salty water.

I claw my way back to the surface and cough for breath. The raft is floating away from me, headed toward the ocean. "Mama!" Mary cries out.

My babies! I crawl and kick through the water, seeing nothing but the raft with my children on top. I close the distance. A final lunge, and I grab onto the wood.

I'm completely exhausted now and start to shiver. I summon my very last bit of energy and scream as loud as I can. "HELP!"

Everyone looks toward me. Irma raises her see-far glasses. Thal acts right away, jumping back into the water and swimming with powerful strokes.

"We'll be alright," I tell my children, as much to calm myself as them.

Mary extends a foot toward me. "Hold on, mama."

That might pull her off the raft, so instead, I slip a hand beneath one of the lines holding the raft's bedding onto the wooden door, and twist the thin rope around my wrist. "I won't let go again. No matter what."

Thal finally reaches us, breathing hard. "Don't worry. Hold on to the raft."

With his strong legs, he tows us toward land. I help as much as I can. Halfway to the shore, Rod and Griff jump into the water and help too.

Thal may not be clever, but he's strong and reliable. Once again, I thank Irma's decision to capture him and convince him to join us. When Mary and Isaac are safe, I hug Thal and kiss him. "Thank you."

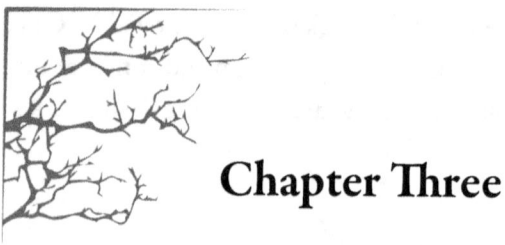

Chapter Three

S afely ashore, we unload in the pre-dawn light. *What now?* I look upstream, envisioning what lies beyond the dark waters and the silhouettes of broken pine trees. My knees tremble.

Seeming to read my mind, Irma says, "We won't go back to the mountains."

Irma and I were born in the forested mountains to the northwest. It's cooler there, especially in the deep stream valleys. Such territory is highly desired—my birth group fought constantly to hold our valley and nearby hunting grounds. Then a fungus destroyed our sweet potatoes—our main crop—and we ate the last of the nearby animals. Our enemies took advantage of our weakness and attacked.

It comes back to me almost every night: I'm eight years old, sitting at the cooking fire at sunset, watching my mother stir the stew. My stomach grumbles—my mother's not only the village healer and keeper of ancient knowledge, she can make even pine bark taste good. With the right herbs, anything's possible.

Suddenly an arrow flies through the air and pierces my mother's throat. She drops the wooden spoon, blood spurts out, her eyes go wide in terror. Men and women from another valley rush into our village. They have scary red and black stripes painted on their cheeks. They swing axes and machetes at our men and older women, and scoop up the younger women and children. I scream and scream and run as fast as I can. One of the attackers is catching up to me. She smells awful. Aunt Irma steps out of her hut with a raised bow and shoots the woman in the face. "Follow me," Irma tells me. "We're outnumbered." She helps me escape, along with her then-young sons.

Sometimes I wonder what happened to the captured children from our village. If they're still alive, they'd be adults or close to it. Do they paint their faces and go on killing raids? Are they slaves? Are they even still alive? In my mind, I often thank Aunt Irma, despite her intolerance and violence, for saving me from such a fate.

We change into our deerskins and moccasins. They're hotter than our woven clothes, but much more durable, and don't collect as many ticks or chiggers. I fashion a sling for Isaac and carry him on my back. Then we search for food. With downed trees and saw-toothed palmettos everywhere, it's hard going.

Where the flood waters have receded, we find dead rats, iguanas, and other small animals among the debris. Unfortunately, they've spoiled in the harsh sun, and are covered with flies and ants.

We move inland and gather berries, grasshoppers, worms, beetle grubs, whatever we can find. Mary and I search areas of broken concrete for catmint and allium. I pass out the leaves to everyone, we crush them, and rub the oils on our skin and clothes to keep ticks and 'skeetos away.

Thal, Rod, and Griff use their ancient machetes and knives to hack apart palmettos. The blades have been sharpened so many times, I wonder how much wider they were when new. Rod and Griff turn it into a contest, as they do with most things. We eat the palmetto hearts and leaf bases raw.

Griff brings me extra helpings, while Rod supplies Angelica. "For Mary and Isaac," Griff tells me. "Can't let them starve."

"Thank you." He and his brother are as unlikable as their mother, but to him as with everyone, group survival comes before all else.

Irma tells Bree and Tash to practice with their bows. "You need to get as good as the rest of us."

I check Angelica's eye injury. The leaf underside is crusted with dried blood and pus. The lids are dark purple and sealed shut. They should bulge outward, but are flat.

"This might hurt," I tell her.

I part the eyelids with my fingers. She whimpers.

It looks worse. Her eye, pink and white with angry red veins, has tilted backward. The torn pupil and iris are half visible beneath the upper eyelid, with a cavern of air above.

"It hurts," she says.

I tie a new plantain leaf over her eye, then give her more willow bark to chew. "You have to lie down till it heals. We'll camp for a while." I'm not sure her eye will heal, and worry that it's 'fected.

The sun is well above the horizon now and it's getting unbearably hot. Soon the temperature will be lethal. "We need shelter," I tell Irma. Not far away, at the crest of the hill, is the half-crumbled red brick building where we stayed before attacking the tower.

She nods. "Let's go."

Thal carries Angelica as we hurry to the building. It's overgrown with vines and small trees.

The basement, which is cooler than the open air, looks as we left it, neatly excavated and mostly clean. The grass mats have disintegrated, but we have the bedding from the rafts. We remove our clothes and check each other for ticks. As always, Rod and Griff leer at me and Angelica when they see us naked, but they know better than to anger Thal, who is much stronger than they are.

I am tired and afraid, but at least we have shelter. As a bonus, we find mice and roaches, which we catch and add to our mid-day stew. The trick to eating roaches and other insects, I've learned, is to pull off the legs and wings so they don't get stuck between your teeth.

AS ALWAYS, WE RISE before dawn. Thal and I coupled during the night, something I really needed. Irma once told me I can't get pregnant while breast feeding, which is good—I can't handle two babies. I feel a little guilty—Angelica tolerates Thal having sex with me and Irma, but doesn't like it. She knows that's the way our group is, though. And he likes her best—she's the youngest and prettiest, and even I want to kiss her sometimes.

The moon is only a sliver, so we have to wait until pre-morning twilight to begin searching for food. We have about three hours before the sun rises high enough to overheat our bodies, which isn't much time.

Thal catches a rat snake in the rubble. Other than that, it's more insects and palmetto hearts. Insects are nutritious, but we need far more than we can find.

When we return, Angelica is moaning and whimpering. "My eye, it hurts more and more."

My belly tenses. Her injury should be getting better, not worse. "Are you chewing the willow bark I gave you?"

"It doesn't help."

I remove the bandage from Angelica's eye and pull apart the purple-bruised eyelids. A rancid stench enters my nose and I wince. Her eye is half collapsed and I can see into the angry red socket. Yellow-green pus drips out.

"I can't see in that eye," Angelica tells me. "Por favor, ayúdame."

I feel her forehead. It's hot, meaning she has a 'fection. I have to act now or she'll die.

I put the leaf back over her eye and tell Irma quietly, "Angelica's wound is 'fected."

Irma winces. "Will she die? Will her baby die?"

"If we don't do something."

Thal says loudly, "This place is cursed too. Angelica is cursed. We should leave her."

Angelica hears him and wails. "Please don't leave me, Thal! Don't leave me, mi amor!"

"Do something," Irma tells me.

I return to Angelica and hold her hand. "We're not going to leave you. But I'm going to have to remove your eye. It's 'fected."

Tears drip from her good eye. "No, you have to save it. Don't take it out. I'll never see right again. And I'll look horrible and mi amor won't lay with me anymore."

Thal—and certainly Rod and Griff—would lay with Angelica regardless, but I keep that thought to myself. "I will make you a permanent eye patch," I say, "and you will still be the most beautiful one in our group."

"Please save my eye, chera."

I sigh. "Do you want to die? Do you want to lose your baby?"

"Los espíritus have cursed me. Is it because I joined your group instead of fighting you off?"

Spirits, curses... "It was an accident," I tell her. "The world is harsh and full of pain, but we just have to deal with it. Now do you want to live or not?"

She nods slightly.

"Then trust me."

I get the medicine pack and sharpen the small cutting knife with the whetstone. I tell Bree to boil some water and keep the fire going. I tell Tash, "We need a sturdy stick, but not too big."

"Why?" she asks.

"For Angelica so she doesn't bite off her tongue."

Angelica stiffens, terror on her face.

"Don't worry," I say. "I'll be quick."

When the blade is sharp enough to slice the skin of my palm without much pressure, I submerge it in the boiling water—my mother told me this prevents 'fections—then wash my hands. I call over Thal and Irma. "Hold her still." There isn't anything strong in the room to tie her to.

I place Tash's stick between Angelica's upper and lower teeth. "Bite down on this."

Irma holds her head still. Thal sits on her thighs and grips her arms.

I pry Angelica's eyelids apart and slice into the muscles holding her ruined eye. Angelica lets out muffled screams and her body convulses, but Irma and Thal hold her steady enough for me to work. I smell piss streaming out of her.

I continue to cut. Although I can skin and gut an animal or fish as well as anyone, I've never performed surgery before. But I've seen it done. When I was a child in my clan's mountain valley, my father, Aunt Irma, and a cousin were attacked while patrolling our borders. Irma and my cousin brought my father back with a blood-soaked bandage over his belly. My mother examined him and said he'd die unless she could sew his guts back together. I watched her try, but in the end, he died anyway, and my mother wept for days. I hope I'll be more successful.

I finish cutting and pull out the half-collapsed eye. The socket is inflamed and putrid. "Keep holding her," I tell Thal and Irma, and dig out the layer of 'fected tissue, fighting not to throw up. It bleeds a lot and Angelica makes horrible gurgling noises.

One of my mother's healing lessons was how to cauterize bad injuries to stop bleeding and 'fection. I put aside the knife and retrieve the tinder spoon. I clean the spoon, grip it by the wooden handle, and place the metal end in the fire, just long enough to heat it. I return to Angelica and place the heated spoon into her eye socket. She screams and thrashes despite the hands gripping her. I yank the spoon away before it plunges into her brain.

"Hold her still!" I shout.

Bree and Tash come over to help Thal and Irma. I reheat the spoon and try again.

It takes several applications to cauter the whole socket, by which time Angelica has passed out. I clean the charred flesh and hope she won't lose her baby.

WE STAY IN THE CRUMBLED brick building for several days while Angelica's eye socket heals. Her baby is still moving inside. I sew the eyelids together with a bone needle and sinew, and make her a patch from deerskin.

Irma announces, "There's not enough food here. The storm wrecked everything. We should move, someplace with game and fresh water."

"Angelica should rest," I say. Her fever has disappeared, but the pain hasn't.

"This place is cursed," Thal says.

I lose my patience. "There are no curses. There are only accidents and poor planning."

Thal raises an eyebrow at me as if I'm stupid. I laugh inside, and must have betrayed a smirk, because he frowns and says, "Do not anger the fates."

I ignore him and ask Irma, "If we're not staying here, where are we going?"

"West, away from the storm damage. Until we find someplace good."

That's not much of a plan. "The really big roads connect old cities," I say. "Plenty of shelter, places we can defend, maybe books and artifacts."

"You and your books again."

"Someplace along a river," I continue. "We can catch fish."

Irma shrugs. "We'll see what we find."

We pack up at nightfall and Irma leads us west, away from the estuario. The nights have returned to cloudlessness, and the moon is half full, giving us plenty of light to see by. I'm in the back of the group with my children and Angelica, who refuses to speak. It's hot and humid, but bearable.

We follow an old road, about 30 footsteps across. Its faded surface is cracked and pitted, with weeds bursting through the cracks and broken branches scattered around. But it isn't choked with saw palmettos and downed trees, and we travel at a steady pace. It's quiet except for faint wind, crickets, and the occasional call of a nightjar.

Angelica waddles along, her bulging belly and missing eye making her clumsy. She trips and nearly falls.

Irma turns and frowns at us. "You have to move faster."

Even with Isaac on my back, I could keep up with the others. But Mary has short footsteps and isn't used to walking long distances, and Angelica is pregnant. I find a slender but sturdy branch by the side of the road and snap off the twigs, then give it to Angelica as a walking stick.

"Gracias." She doesn't smile though—she hasn't smiled since the storm.

"We can carve it when we stop," I say. "Take off the bark and add some designs."

Thal picks up Mary and puts her on his broad shoulders, gripping her legs to hold her on. "I'll carry you a while."

"Thank you daddy!" she squeals. "I can see far up here!"

When the horizon begins to glow behind us and day birds begin their brief flurry of activity, Irma sends her children out to forage for food, accompanied by Thal. I tell Angelica to rest and she sits. Irma and I continue down the road, searching for shelter. I carry Isaac on my back and walk slowly enough for Mary to keep up.

We pass over another wide road that runs from southwest to northeast. It's astonishing how the people of the Vanished World could build roads that cross over each other and last so long.

Our road leads to a sprawling complex of three-story red-brick buildings. Most of the trees between them have been toppled by the storm, and debris is strewn everywhere. But other than broken windows, the larger buildings are still intact. In the distance, I see a tower that's much wider than the one we used to live in.

"That's perfect!" I tell Irma. At least until the estuario marsh recovers. And maybe it has books, like our tower. Maybe some of them can tell us how to build boats or machines, or more about the Vanished Ones, what they were like and why they disappeared.

Irma examines the tower through her see-far glasses. From the few times I've used them, they magnify distant objects by tenfold and brighten them a little.

Irma points at one of the lower windows. "It's occupied."

She's right. There's a white wisp of smoke curling out the window. By the size and color, it's someone's cooking fire.

"We should scout this place tomorrow night," Irma says. "Let's go back and find another place for today."

I want to stay as far as possible from other groups. Horrible memories surface again, causing my whole body to clench. My mother slaughtered in front of me. Running from painted-face killers, terrified what they might do if they caught me. I also remember how we massacred Angelica's group.

Irma peers at me and exhales, as if she's reading my thoughts and finds them irritating.

We return to Angelica and the rest of our group, then search for shelter. We find an intact basement within a cluster of wrecked buildings just off the road. Thal has shot a rabbit buck, and we make a stew with rabbit meat, grubs, palmetto hearts, and dandelions.

"No sign of deer," Thal grumbles. "Not even dogs."

Irma tells everyone about the settlement at the end of the road.

"Do they have women?" Rod asks.

"We'll find out," Irma says.

Thal tells her sons, "You must be nice to any women you meet. You must win their heart, not treat it like a battle."

I ignore the males. "We should circle around that place," I tell Irma. "It could be dangerous."

"Through the torn-up forest?" Irma says. "We may be caught without shelter when the sun rises high enough to cook us."

"We should follow the road," Thal says, "and see what it brings."

Irma nods. "There can't be too many people there, or we'd have seen them by now. We saw only one cooking fire. Thal, Lucy, and I will go estimate their strength, and how we might defeat them if we have to fight."

"My father was killed scouting," I mention.

"He was my kin too. I was there—I remember. I also remember how the Painted Ones took us by surprise and killed almost everyone in our clan. I never want to be surprised again."

I nod in agreement.

After we eat, I whisper to Angelica, "If I don't return, please take care of Mary and Isaac."

She squeezes my hand. "Please return, chera."

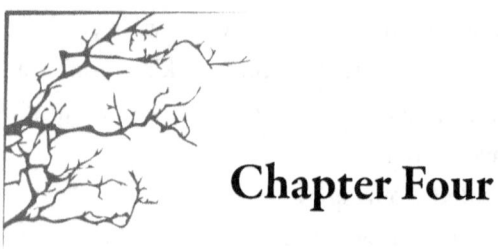

Chapter Four

The next night, Irma, Thal, and I return to the area of three-story buildings and the big tower. My heart pounds so hard, I almost wonder if others can hear it. My skin turns cold and clammy. I have my bow out, fingers pressing an arrow against the string. Irma and Thal have their bows out also, but don't look worried. All three of us carry machetes for close combat.

It's quiet. I see no fires or other signs of people. Nor do I see any animals or edible plants.

We take a pathway off the main road, heading west through a wreckage of pines and sweetgums. Brick buildings are visible here and there through gaps in the trees. Whenever Irma stops to look through her see-far glasses, we strain our ears for sounds of trouble. Just faint wind rustling the treetops and distant crickets, no voices or footsteps.

We come to a section of trees that extend so far to the north, we can't see through them. Irma puts up a hand and points in that direction. The trees will supply cover to approach the tower, as long as we're careful not to step on any twigs.

We move slowly and carefully, closer and closer to the unseen tower. I hear leaves rustle to the left, stop and spin to face it. Something dark is creeping toward us. It's lower to the ground than a human. I put up a hand, then point.

Thal points to the right. Another shape jumps over a log and disappears in the underbrush. We form a tight circle, each covering a third of the woods, bows ready.

I hear growling. A coyote, or a large dog. Dogs are more dangerous because they travel in large packs and coordinate their attacks.

Thal whispers, "Come to me, walking meat."

A large, dark brown dog—not a coyote—emerges from the shadows in front of me. Ears back, it displays a mouth full of sharp teeth. It barks, low and loud.

All around us, more dogs bark. Then they attack, dashing toward us.

I release my arrow. It hits the big dog in the chest. It yelps and crashes to the ground.

I hear two more yelps. Thal and Irma must have hit also.

Fangs clamp onto my right leg. Another dog, a little shorter and thinner, with tan fur. My deer hide pants are too thick for its teeth to pierce—at least for now.

I sling my bow over my shoulder—can't afford to lose it—and pull out my machete. The dog tears at my pants, trying to reach the flesh beneath.

I swing the machete down, cutting deep into the dog's neck, all the way to the spine. Blood spurts out, soaking my tunic. The dog wobbles and collapses, but its teeth are stuck in my pants, and the half-severed head won't let go. I pry it off with my machete, slicing through the snout in the process.

I hear scuffling and cursing from Thal and Irma, and the yelps of injured dogs. I don't turn to look; I keep my eyes on my third of the forest.

No more dogs attack, as if they've accepted defeat. I risk a glance over my shoulder at Irma. "Are they gone?"

"Yes," Thal says, "and we have meat for many days."

An arrow flies through the trees and strikes Thal in the shoulder, passing through his buckskin vest. He stares at it with surprise on his face. I want to scream, but can't even do that.

Then my legs take over and I dodge behind a tree. Irma and Thal do the same. More arrows fly toward us, but miss. I can't see who's shooting at us, how many, or where exactly they are.

"Run," I shout, even though I'm not in charge. I sheathe my machete so I won't slash myself if I trip over one of the downed logs or branches. Thal yanks out the arrow and yells in pain.

We charge south through the forest, not worrying about stealth. My leg hurts where the dog bit, even though it didn't break the skin.

Thal grunts behind me. I hear dogs barking—they're running after us, knowing we're afraid. I wonder if the archers are also following us, and if the dogs are trained. As long as we keep a steady pace, though, we can stay ahead of them.

Thal is normally faster than me, but he doesn't pass me. Besides being injured, he's extremely protective.

We exit the tangled forest, onto an old blacktop full of cracks and weeds. It's faster going here, and I cross a paved road into a jumble of wrecked buildings. We can lose our pursuers here, maybe even ambush them.

I hear a scream of pain behind me, followed by a snap and a thud. I halt and look back.

Thal is lying face down on the ground. Has he been shot again? I don't see an arrow sticking out. Irma rushes over to help and so do I.

An old piece of rusty rebar juts from the top of his right moccasin and pins his foot to the ground. His leg lies at an unnatural angle and a jagged bone protrudes from the side of his ankle. Blood gushes from the injuries. Thal's face is contorted in agony.

Irma and I pull Thal's foot off the rebar, trying not to mangle it even more. He grits his teeth. "Hurry."

We hear barking dogs, then a faint voice from that direction, "Follow the dogs."

Irma and Thal lock eyes. Their faces turn grim. I know what they're thinking, because I'm thinking it too. We won't escape with Thal unable to run.

"We need to find someplace we can defend ourselves," I say. "Or hide."

"We can't hide from dogs," Irma says. "They'll sniff us out."

"Then we take cover and fight."

"No," Thal says. "Return to the others."

"Without you?" Irma asks.

"You're too hurt to fight alone," I tell him.

Thal's eyes blaze in anger. "The children won't survive if we all die. Go. I'll hold them off." On his good leg, he hops behind a pile of rubble, then draws his bow.

Irma nods and turns to me. "Let's go."

"We can't leave him!" Although he's right—what would happen to Mary and Isaac if I die? Tears blur my sight.

Irma grabs my arm and pushes me forward. I wipe my eyes and scan the broken ground ahead as I run—I don't want to end up like Thal.

I hear barks and growls behind, followed by the twang of a bow and a dog yelp. Another twang, and a human scream, more high-pitched than Thal's voice. Swishes of flying arrows. Thal grunts loudly, followed by sliding rocks and a crash.

I can't help but look back. Thal is on the ground, an arrow in his upper chest. Dogs pounce on him and tear at his exposed neck and hands. He screams in pain. The largest of the dogs thrusts its jaws beneath his vest, shakes its head violently, and pulls out entrails.

Irma grips my arm again, hard, and pulls me along. As we flee, I retch bile into my mouth and nearly choke before spitting it out.

BACK ON THE ROAD, IRMA slaps her shaved head over and over. "They used dogs. We lost Thal because they were smarter. That's never happening again."

Tears roll down my cheeks. I can't stop seeing Thal screaming as his entrails are torn out. I shouldn't have let us approach the other group. I always think the right thing, but never do the right thing.

We return to the others. I let Irma announce that Thal has been killed.

Angelica drops to her knees and wails. "Mi amor, mi amor..."

Bree, Tash, and Mary cry too. Even Rod and Griff stand motionless with open mouths and blinking eyes.

Angelica rises to her feet and stabs a finger at Irma and me. "You just left him to die?"

"It was his decision," Irma says. "His leg was broken and he couldn't run."

"He died to save Irma and me," I add. But without him, everyone knows, our group is much weaker. And I'll miss him. He was so brave, and so devoted to us.

"I want my daddy back," Mary cries in my arms.

I try to comfort her. "I know."

"We must move," Irma says after a while. I agree.

We take the lower road northeast. It's the wrong direction, but we have no choice. Everyone is quiet and sullen. Angelica cries a lot.

I'm feeling down myself and tire of comforting her. "We need to focus on survival," I tell her. "You have to be strong."

We reach an intersection with a north-south road and take that north. The sun begins to rise. We search for shelter and find another basement. We are not as far away from the other group as I would like, so I cut a palmetto leaf and use it as a broom to sweep away our footprints.

My stomach growls but there is nothing to eat. I try to breast feed Isaac, but don't have much milk to give him.

Rod and Griff argue over who gets to replace Thal and who gets to have sex with who. Irma slaps each of them in the head. "Lucy is your first cousin and Angelica is carrying a child."

"I need a woman," Rod says. Griff points a thumb at his chest. "Me too."

"You'll have to wait," Irma answers.

I hold Mary and Isaac close to me and sing them to sleep.

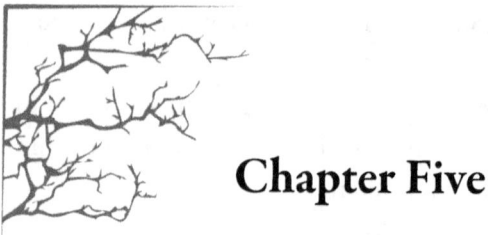

Chapter Five

The next night, we continue north, then head west on the widest road I've ever seen, over fifty footsteps across. There's a low wall in the middle. Taking the north half of the road, we're harder to see and harder to reach.

The pine trees that haven't been knocked down by the storm are blackened from past fires. The understory has no palmettos, only freshly sprouted wiregrass and pine seedlings, coaxed forth by the rain. I neither see nor hear anything bigger than a cricket.

"Why is there no game?" Griff asks Irma.

"Keep looking," she tells him, and passes him the see-far glasses.

I'm not surprised. Between fires, storms, scorching heat, and desperate humans and canines, it's no wonder we haven't seen a single deer since we left the tower. This wasteland won't even support rabbits or squirrels. No place to hide from the murderous sun, and no water to drink or cool the body.

Eventually, though, a road this wide should lead to a city of the Vanished Ones. Shelter will be easier to find, and maybe books and other useful things. And maybe we'll find people who can read, who've brought back some of the Vanished World knowledge, and will accept us into their group instead of trying to kill us.

Going by the number of ruined buildings I've seen during my life, the Vanished Ones were far more numerous than people today. They must have gotten along, been able to cooperate. And the more people working together, the more they could accomplish. I'd like to learn their secret—and why they disappeared.

After an hour of walking, I notice human bones scattered alongside the road, an adult and a child. Looking closer, they've been gnawed on. By coyotes? Dogs? Not humans, I hope. I've never encountered cannibals, but parents in my birth village warned their children never to wander too far away or crazy people might eat them.

When the first glow of morning appears in the east, accompanied by the brief singing of chickadees and pine warblers, Irma sends her offspring to gather whatever food they can find. Irma and I search for shelter. I leave Mary with Angelica, but carry Isaac in a sling on my back.

We find no buildings of any kind, not even ruined ones, just an endless expanse of burned and storm-shattered pine trees. I miss my birth home in the mountain valley, which was cool enough to survive outside during the day. I miss the safety of the estuario tower, and all the food we had before the storm.

We spot a broken bridge ahead, a road overpass that's collapsed. It's not enough shelter to keep us alive—we need a place below the surface, with the cooling of thick soil and rocks. But where there are road crossings, old buildings are usually nearby.

I point north. "That way?"

Irma nods.

Just past the road intersection, collapsed buildings lie to the left and right. We search through the wreckage, but can't find any basements. The sun rises above the horizon. We're running out of time.

I see a last possibility. Trenches have been dug on either side of the road, with metal-lined tunnels running beneath the entrances to the building lots. The tunnel on the left has collapsed, but the one on the right is intact, and is clear of debris—probably flushed downstream by the storm. And it's wide enough to crawl into, although barely.

I scan the horizons carefully. I don't want to drown in one of these tunnels, but no clouds are visible.

We return to the others. Griff is cursing and shaking out his pants. His ankles and lower legs are covered with angry red welts.

"He stepped on a fire ant nest," Rod explains, "and didn't notice till it was too late."

I tell everyone as we return to the road intersection, "Gather any plantain leaves you see and give them to Griff for his legs." I don't have enough left, and even if I did, wouldn't waste them on Griff's ant bites.

At the collapsed overpass, Bree unpacks the iron pan we brought from the tower, and fries the pine seeds, slivers of inner whitebark, and the insects everyone collected. Still hungry afterward, we crawl into the metal tube, one at a time. The bottom is damp and cool to the touch. If it rains, I hope we'll have enough time to get out.

THAT NIGHT, WE CONTINUE west on the wide road, finding nothing but more burned and storm-wrecked forest. I can't produce enough milk for Isaac, and yearn for animals or fish to eat. Isaac screams a lot.

"Quiet your child," Irma tells me.

My body tenses, but she's right—enemies might hear us. "We need food."

Rod lets out a huff. "We know that already."

I ignore him and go to one of the trees that's still alive. With my knife, I cut into the bark and peel off long strips. The outer bark is charred but the inner bark is still white and tender.

The others join me and we fry enough to fill our empty bellies. I chew some into a paste and feed it to Isaac, which quiets him—at least for now.

We return to the road. It seems to go on forever, with no sign of the Vanished Ones city I hoped for.

"We should have stayed at the estuario," I say. By now, the marsh should be recovering.

Irma stomps over and slaps me hard on the cheek. "Shut up."

The sudden pain brings flashes of light. I hate Irma and want her dead. My fist flies out and hits her in the nose.

Irma stares at me more with surprise than pain—my punches aren't very strong. Then her face flares with anger. She's going to hurt me, bad.

I back up and grip the hilt of my machete.

Irma whips her machete out of its scabbard and points the blade at me. Rod and Griff pull their blades out too.

Isaac's strapped to my back. Next to me, Mary wails in terror.

Rod and Griff approach with their machetes. Their eyes narrow with vindictiveness, but their mouths curve into leers. "I don't care if you're a cousin," Rod says. "We're the men now."

"Leave her alone!" Angelica shouts. Everyone ignores her.

No choice now. I pull out my machete, but there's no way I can defeat all three of them, or even two of them. "Not in front of my children," is all I can think to say.

"Everyone stop!" Irma shouts. "Put your blades away!"

Her sons hesitate, then follow her order. I re-sheath my machete, but continue to back toward the trees.

"You can't survive on your own," Irma tells me.

I remember the gnawed bones we passed yesterday. One was a child. Unfortunately, Irma's right—every predator in the world would see my children as easy pickings.

"You need me, too," I say. I'm the only healer—and the only one trying to bring back the knowledge of the Vanished Ones, who were like gods compared to us.

"You should teach everyone how to heal," she says, "not just Mary."

And make myself replaceable? "Mother-daughter tradition," I use as an excuse.

Irma glares at me. "If you ever point a weapon at me or my sons again, I'll take your other ear. Or maybe your nose."

Am I not allowed to fight back? But at least she stopped her vile sons from raping me—for now. When the group continues down the road, I follow at a safe distance.

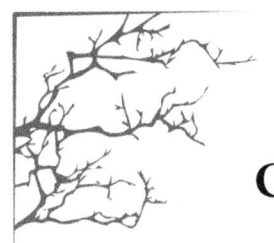

Chapter Six

The road ends at a collapsed bridge. A green sign next to the road reads 'Lake Oconee.' I don't see a lake, but a river runs through the middle of the bridge wreckage, flanked by young red maples and sweetgums.

Drinking water is the first priority. We fill our pots and flasks, but river water has to be boiled or it could make us sick. Tash starts a fire.

I hear a woodpecker hammering bark, then spot it on one of the dead trees. White underside, black and white wings and back, red crest—a red-bellied woodpecker according to my bird book back in the tower.

Bree raises her bow and impales the bird with an arrow. "Good shot!" Irma tells her.

A single bird won't even feed Bree. I find a suitable branch and tie my fishing line and hook to it. I rest it on the river bank and dig for worms to use as bait. Early morning is the most productive time to fish, and I don't want to waste any of that time searching for bait.

"We'll do that," Irma says. "Go look for shelter."

"By myself?"

"You're good at it. And you're careful."

"Can I have the see-far glasses?"

She pulls them off and hands them to me. The joined black tubes are thick, and feel sturdy.

"Don't let your sons come after me," I say.

"They'll stay here, fishing. But they have needs I can't control forever. As long as you're not in your fertile period, you should take turns with them till Angelica's available again, or we find someone else. It's for the best of everyone."

The thought horrifies me—especially since I've known them since they were born. "What if I don't want to?"

"Why wouldn't you? They're old enough, and have no diseases."

Because I don't like them, I want to say. And I am not anyone's plaything.

"I'll tell them to do it the way you want," she says. "You'll get used to it."

The way I want is for those rapists to keep away. But Irma's siding with them. I wave my daughter over. "Come look for shelter with me." I'll take Isaac too and leave the group.

Irma says, "Mary and Isaac stay here. They'll slow you."

"No they won't."

"They stay here." Her face hardens into the familiar look of, 'if you speak again, I'll hit you.' She's probably guessed my plan.

"I wanna go with mama," Mary insists.

"It's safer if you stay with the group," Irma tells her. "She'll be back soon."

"What if I can't find anything before sunrise?" I ask Irma. "Will you be here so I can find you again?" I tell Mary, and anyone else who might not know, "The river can keep you from overheating if you take off your moccasins and stick your feet in the water. Hands too."

Irma lets out a huff. "I taught *you* that, Lucy. I'll keep your children safe. We might not be here, but we'll be along the river. Now go find shelter—sleeping in the open is too dangerous, even with flowing water."

"Be careful," Angelica tells me as I leave.

I take a cracked, overgrown road that follows the river north, stopping now and then to look through the see-far glasses. The Vanished Ones built most of their houses and other structures along roads, so I expect to find something suitable eventually. As I walk, I think about ways to escape Irma and her sons. I wish I could kill them, but even Griff is a better fighter than me. All that practice fighting his brother, I suppose.

I find ruined houses set back from the road, but none have basements or other suitable shelter. I continue north, pass an intersection with an east-west road, and come to another downed bridge.

Irritated, I return to the intersection and take the east road. Not for the first time, I wonder what my life would be like if I'd been born in the Vanished World. No worries about food, water, or shelter. Millions and millions of people, cooperating instead of fighting, reading books and writing. I'd be a healer with advanced machines that could cure any injury or sickness. The air would be cool enough to work during the day. Plants and animals would thrive everywhere. People would know everything about them, and live in harmony with them.

The eastern horizon begins to glow. I walk faster. I find big mounds of charred timber covered with kudzu vines. They're useless as shelter. But I spot a snare trap. It's empty, unfortunately, but it means another group is nearby.

My eyes and ears strain for movement. I consider fleeing back to Irma and the others, but continue east.

I hear banging and tapping noises ahead. I recognize it from past repair work on our tower and floating walkway. Someone is hammering nails into wood. I head that direction, using surviving trees as cover.

I hear low voices and smell meat cooking. My mouth salivates. I wonder what they're cooking, and how much they have. What if these people are friendly? Or at least not murderous? They can't be worse than Irma and her sons, can they?

I come to a grassy field crowded with lichen-splotched stone grave markers. Beyond is a long brick building surrounded by cracked blacktop and grass. Keeping cover behind a tree, I scan the area carefully through the see-far glasses, then rotate the middle knob to bring the building in focus.

The building's side windows curve at the top and hold colored glass that's still intact. The slanting roof is a patchwork of old and new, with a chest-high wall of thin logs along the edge. Partly visible, a man and two women are fixing a big hole near the building's entrance, which faces an old road. A wisp of smoke rises from between the walls, the source of the delicious smell.

Should I try to talk to them? Join them if they'll let me? My children are back with Irma, but I can retrieve them afterward. My legs tremble—I don't know what to do.

I take a deep breath and force my fear away. I can't live under Irma anymore. I'm going to act.

I hide my bow, machete, carving knife, and see-far glasses in a patch of underbrush, then walk into the graveyard with palms raised in front, showing that I'm unarmed. One of the women working on the roof spots me and shouts. The man climbs down a ladder, disappearing into the building. The two women raise bows and point arrows at me.

I keep walking forward. I could change my mind and run away, using the gravestones as partial cover. But I may never get another chance like this. I should have done this with Angelica's group.

The man exits a door facing the road. He is around Thal's size and age—when Thal was still alive—but with a longer beard. He looks well-fed, wears a vest and skirt made from woven grass, and holds a smooth pole with center and rear grips and a curved blade at the end. He's followed by a pale old man, also wearing grass clothes and holding a similar weapon. He has a long white beard and tied-back hair. Like Angelica, the old man wears a metal cross around his neck.

We approach each other, me with my palms still up.

"Kneel," the younger man says. The curved blade at the end of his weapon looks sharp enough to slice off my head.

I kneel, palms still out. "My name's Lucy."

Their eyes scan me, then the broken forest beyond.

"I'm starving," I continue. "Can I join you?"

The old man laughs. "Where's the rest of your group? You don't expect us to believe you're out here by yourself, do you?"

I respond with partial truth. "I was in another group, but I ran away. Then I got lost."

"Why'd you run away?" the old man says.

"The matriarch wanted to give me to her sons against my will." My skin burns at the memory.

The old man looks at the younger man. "She seems harmless enough. Certainly is skinny. Let's bring her inside."

The younger man searches me for weapons and finds that I have none. He rubs a finger against my vest but his eyes and mouth don't show that he wants me, just that he's curious.

"Deer?" he asks.

"Yes."

"From where? I haven't seen one in years."

"It's old." We'd brought deerskins from the mountains and had killed a few before settling at the tower. Most places were too hot for them.

"What happened to your ear?"

Again, the truth will work. "Punishment from the matriarch."

"For what?"

Irma and I had always disagreed on things, but after our slaughter of the prior tower inhabitants—the three adults, anyway—I tried to convince Thal to never agree to such a thing again. I pleased and flattered him, then told him it wasn't right to kill people just because we wanted something they had. But he laughed and called me foolish, saying, "what's next, don't eat rabbits or fish?" Irma found out and accused me of plotting against her, then made an example of me.

The man is waiting for an answer. "We have different views of the world," I say.

He shrugs and ushers me through the door. Inside is a long room. Big logs hold up the roof beams, which are topped by mismatched boards except in the damaged section. A wooden ladder leads to the hole. A more permanent ladder is attached to the back wall, leading to an open hatch.

Old wooden benches line the walls, piled with tools, inked parchments, and decorations. The rising sun casts beams of blue and red through the east windows, forming multicolored patches on the concrete floor.

My attention fixes on the big stove in the center of the room, the source of smoke I saw. Unlike ours—before the storm destroyed it—their stove is surrounded by piled-up rocks, presumably for insulation. And it has an interior chamber for roasting.

An elderly dark-skinned woman thrusts a forked stick into the oven shelf and removes a browned rabbit, followed by another. They smell delicious. A lanky teenage girl stirs an iron cauldron on the stove top, rich with the smell of cooked roots and herbs. Four children, skin every shade of brown, play with little plastic figures from the Vanished World.

Everyone turns and stares at me. I hear the two women with bows walking on the roof. They haven't climbed down or resumed hammering, meaning they're still on alert.

"Who's this?" the old woman asks.

I've never seen a face with so many creases. She wears a metal cross similar to the old man's.

"Says she's alone and starving," the old man responds.

"My name is Lucy," I tell everyone. "I'm a healer, and carry no sickness."

"I'm Hannah," the old woman says. No one else gives their name. She points at my tattoos. "Why do you have airplanes on your arms?"

That must be a word for flying machines. "As a reminder that even the impossible is possible."

Hannah smiles. "Eat with us." She hands me a wooden bowl and spoon. The teenage girl scoops root stew out of the cauldron and into everyone's bowls. The oldest two children cut up the rabbit meat and hand out pieces. The ones in front of me drop the meat into their bowls.

When it's my turn, I shove the rabbit meat into my mouth. It's the best thing I've eaten in weeks.

"We raise them," Hannah says.

"What?"

"Rabbits. They breed incredibly fast, and eat the plants we cut around the church."

"We grew sweet potatoes when I was a child," I say. "Never thought of raising rabbits."

The old man slings a bow over his shoulder and passes bowls of food up to the women on the roof. Then he joins them. "I'll watch the west."

The younger man sits at a bench by the door, one eye on me and one eye on the door, long weapon at his feet. Hannah, the teenage girl, and four children sit cross-legged on the floor in a circle.

I join the circle. If these people were going to kill me, they wouldn't waste food on me. I eat my stew fast in case they change their mind and I have to run.

Hannah asks lots of questions, and everyone listens.

I don't mention our tower or how we killed most of the original occupants. "We've been wandering, but the forest is burned and storm-damaged, and there's nothing to eat."

"We do have troubles with fires," Hannah says. "That's why we keep the area around the church clear of trees and shrubs."

A church. That explains the colored glass in the windows, which have circular pictures in the middle that are too grimy and sunlit to make out. I've seen churches before, but they're usually burnt. Except for the roof hole—maybe a storm casualty—this one is completely intact.

"A friend in my old group," I say, "wears a cross a little like yours."

"She's a believer?"

"She prays to the spirits of the Vanished World. At least she used to."

Hannah frowns and touches her cross. "That's not what this means. It's a symbol of hope, that God will deliver the souls of the faithful from this cursed world, deliver us into paradise."

My mother believed something like that, although she didn't have a cross, and rarely talked about it. It never really made sense to me.

Hannah finishes her bowl of food—she's the last to finish—and goes to a recessed area in the back of the room. The floor there is raised, and crowded with old chairs and other furniture. She returns with two books, different from the ones in our tower.

"Can you read?" she asks.

My breath catches. She's offering new books to read. "A little."

She passes me one titled *Holy Bible*. "This is the Bible. The revelations of God. If you stay, I'll teach it to you. It connects us to the past and to the divine."

"You can teach me to read? Better, I mean?"

"I'd be glad to." She hands me the other book, *The Infernocene: How We Ended the World*. "This tells how humanity destroyed the Earth out of ignorance and greed. They cut down the forests, wiped out the animals, and poisoned the air and water. They knew the harm they were causing, but chose not to stop it. Then once they decided, half-heartedly, to take action, it was too late. The changes happened too fast to control—hotter and hotter temperatures, rising seas, massive fires, storms and floods, and the ground itself exploding in the far north. Crops failed and diseases killed millions and millions. The clouds—there used to be clouds almost everywhere—disappeared almost entirely, which made it even hotter. And instead of working together, people fought each other for what was left."

I stare at her, searching for some clue that she's lying. "That can't be true. The Vanished Ones were gods compared to us."

"They were just people. Just as flawed as us, only more numerous, and able to cause more damage." Hannah taps a brown finger against *The Infernocene*. "The fuels they burned to power their civilization destabilized the balance that made civilization possible in the first place. And they started wars for no sane reason, using weapons more destructive than you can imagine."

Her eyes are sincere. And I can barely read—who am I to say she's wrong? Her words echo inside my head and shatter everything they touch, my entire lifetime of dreams.

She sighs. "We have a lot of books that tell the same story. Too many people lost touch with the world, lost touch with the divine, cared only about themselves and their immediate families. They refused to listen to anything that might inconvenience their comfortable lives, and lived in big tribes that believed everything they did was good and everything others did was bad."

My shattered dream world crumbles to dust. The Vanished Ones were no better than us—maybe worse. "They built roads, cities, flying machines... how could they not solve problems they made themselves?"

"Cleverness is not the same as wisdom," Hannah says, "and the loudest voices are not always the smartest."

A world run by Irmas and Thals. Or worse—at least Irma and Thal tried to keep our group alive. All my ideas about bringing back the Vanished World—why bother?

Hannah's lined face droops with sadness. "The world was once a paradise. Now it's too hot everywhere except the polar and mountain regions, and there, I heard as a girl, groups fight until they kill each other off."

My fingers shake as familiar images appear in my mind—painted killers rushing into my birth village, slaughtering the adults, tying up the children. An arrow flies into my mother's throat and she coughs up blood. I try to shake away the memories, but I've never been able to. They haunt me like some great stalking beast.

Hannah taps the cover of the first book. "According to the Bible, humans have always acted that way. God created the world as a paradise, but the first humans angered Him and were cursed. We must have angered Him even more to receive our current punishment." She taps the second book. "Or we did it to ourselves. Either way, our ancestors made our lives much more difficult than theirs."

My shoulders slump. Life could have been so much better. Instead, the whole world is ruined and murderous. There's no escape—we're cursed.

No... I refuse to believe in curses. Maybe we can learn from the mistakes of the Vanished Ones.

"You said you have more books than these?" I ask.

"Yes, but you should start with the Bible and the other books about spirituality and morality. You seem like a good person, but even I, old as I am, learn more every time I study the Bible, the Dhammapada, and the others."

Maybe there's no real escape, but this place is close enough. My belly is full, and these people are surviving into old age. Instead of killing me, they fed me. And they can read. I wonder how I can sneak Mary and Isaac away from Irma and her sons. And Angelica—can I bring her too?

The old man and two women climb down from the roof. "It's getting too hot to stay outside," the man says.

"No sign of strangers," one of the women says.

I follow the others through a back door, which has a wooden latch on the inside, then down concrete stairs into a dim basement, lit only by tiny, widely spaced windows just below the ceiling. The basement is big and clean, and noticeably cooler than the room above. The beds are layered straw mats with sewn rabbit furs on top, and look comfortable.

At the far end of the room, long wooden boxes with metal-grate doors are stacked nearly to the ceiling. They smell faintly of urine and straw. I see rabbits moving around inside. The teenage girl and two of the children hurry over and feed them dry grass and weeds.

The younger man unlatches a door next to the stairs and tells me, "You go in there."

It's a tiny windowless room with a big pile of straw in one corner and neatly cut wood filling most of the rest. "Why?"

"We don't know you."

I look at Hannah. She says, "Trust takes time. I hope you will forgive us."

The man locks me in. I clear some floor space and spread out the straw. I don't like being their prisoner, but at least I'm alive. I have to decide whether to stay or leave. If I want to leave, will they let me? And if I stay, how will I sneak my children away from Irma?

I HEAR RUSTLING AND muffled voices, and smell food cooking. I'd been dreaming about my mother again, only this time, we were living in a city of the Vanished Ones. Painted-face killers swarmed the smooth streets and smashed their way into our house. They were doing that everywhere, breaking into every home in the world, sparing no one, nor any other living creature.

I have to focus on the present. I have to rescue Mary and Isaac from Irma. She's probably keeping them alive and fed, but they need their mother and I need them. Maybe I could convince the church people to attack Irma and her sons, but there aren't enough of them, and I doubt they would be so foolish. I have to convince them to let me go and come back.

The door unlatches and opens. The younger man, who never gave his name, beckons me out.

I smooth my rumpled hair. "I'm Lucy."

"I know."

I persist. "What's your name?"

"Nathan." He leads me upstairs. It's night, but the full moon and bright stars cast plenty of light through the windows and roof hole. I spot one of the women up there, bow in hand. The other woman and the old man must be up there too—I don't see them in the room. Nathan and I grab bowls and head for the oven.

The stew is just like the morning's, except the rabbit is replaced by mushrooms and beetle grubs. I sit next to Hannah and reintroduce myself to the children and teenager.

"I'm Phoebe," the teenage girl says. The other children are named Estrella, Ray, Adlai, and Krista.

I eat quickly and tell everyone, "I have a daughter named Mary. She's four. And a baby named Isaac. I need to get them."

Everyone stares at me.

"You didn't say you had children," Nathan says.

"Of course they're welcome," Hannah says. "Where did you leave them, and why?"

My throat closes and I have to force out the words. "The matriarch has them. She knew I might run away."

"How do we know this woman's not a spy?" Nathan announces. "She could go back to her group and plan an attack."

"I'm not a spy," I say. "But Mary and Isaac need me."

They ask lots of questions—how big is my group, what kind of weapons do they have, how will I get my children back.

"My group has only three fighters left," I say. "But it would be a bad idea to attack them. I'll go back, then sneak away with my children when everyone is asleep during the day. We'll walk in the river to stay cool. The church isn't far from the river."

"Fifteen minutes through the woods," Phoebe says. "We fish there sometimes and hunt for turtles."

Nathan eyes me and grunts. "We must discuss this. In the meantime, you can help us repair the roof."

"Let me give her a reading lesson first," Hannah says. "Then I'll send her up."

Nathan shrugs and climbs the ladder with a hammer and bow. Hannah and Phoebe coax the four children over to the bench with the inked parchments. The children sit on the floor before the bench. Directed by Phoebe, they open books, dip large feathers into pots of ink, and copy letters from the books onto blank parchments. Phoebe goes from child to child, pronouncing words and explaining meanings. I wonder again if we can do better than the Vanished Ones—if under people like Hannah, we can learn wisdom and put it in practice.

Hannah waves me over to another bench and sits next to me with the Bible. She reads to me, pointing at each word so I can associate the letters with the sounds. "In the beginning when God created the heavens and the earth, the earth was a formless void and darkness covered the face of the deep."

As the book continues, God creates the sky, land, seas, and swarms of plants, animals, and fish of every kind. "Most of them are extinct now," Hannah says. "God must be disappointed that the descendants of Adam and Eve destroyed His work. It's no wonder we're damned."

My clan matriarch from childhood had told this creation story—at least a version she remembered. We didn't have any books for comparing.

"What about *The Infernocene*?" I ask. "Does it also have a creation story?"

"It tells only of destruction. But we have a geology book that describes the formation of the Earth long, long ago. We can look at it another time. Why don't you go help the others with the roof? They'd appreciate it."

I climb the ladder, hoping these people will let me and my children stay. Three empty bowls are stacked by the top. A walkway circles the edge of the roof, just inside the chest-high wall. Even though it's built with narrow logs, the wall looks solid—nailed to cross boards and braced against the roof beams.

The women introduce themselves as Susanna and Magda. The old man is named Abraham. It doesn't seem like anyone's in charge, which is strange.

Susanna and Abraham stand watch with their bows. It's a good position—their archers can take cover behind the encircling wall, but an attacker would have to cross a hundred yards of open ground.

I pass Nathan and Magda pieces of wood and hold them while they drive in nails. They don't trust me with a hammer.

"What happened to your roof?" I ask.

"Big storm," Magda says, "It knocked down the steeple and tore away the roof around it."

Probably the same storm that half-destroyed our tower. "Are you putting the steeple back?" I ask.

"No, we needed the wood." She stops talking after that.

Below, Hannah and Phoebe exit the church, carrying two of the poles with curved blades. They swing them in half circles just above the ground, slicing through grass and weeds—presumably to feed the rabbits. Maybe that's the main purpose of those strange-looking weapons.

I think I see movement in the trees, but no one else notices, and when I look harder, it's gone. Could it be Irma or one of her sons? Or a coyote or dog? I hope it's an animal, and if it's someone from Irma's group, that they didn't recognize me from such a distance.

Should I warn these people, just in case? I don't want them to die like Angelica's group. And whose side would I take if Irma attacked? I hate Irma sometimes, but she's family, and saved me from the painted-face killers. And she has my children.

I won't have to decide—Irma won't attack a position as strong as this. She'll set up an ambush instead, like with Angelica's group.

"Have you ever fought others?" I ask Magda quietly when Nathan goes down to get more wood.

She puts down her hammer. "Why do you ask?"

"You act like you have."

"You're the first outsider we've seen in years. But we're not stupid. Why do you think we stand up here with bows? Even a rabbit can't get close."

"Don't come with me when I get my children," I say. "It's too dangerous."

Magda peers at me. "You put us in a bad position. If we let you leave, don't come back until your group is long gone."

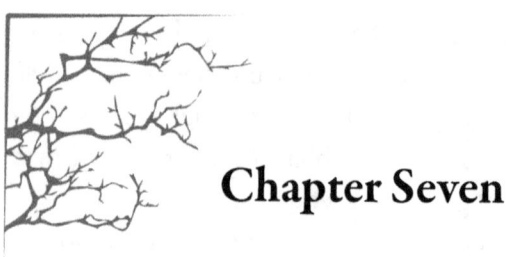

Chapter Seven

A loud crash rouses me from sleep. I blink away the latest nightmare and leap to my feet, scattering bed straw in the process. I'm locked in the storage room again—they still don't trust me during sleeping hours.

Outside my door, a man screams, "Everyone up! We're being attacked!" It sounds like Nathan.

A woman howls, "Rod, right! Griff, left! Daughters, bows!"

It's Irma! How'd they get here in the middle of the day, when the body overheats with the slightest exertion and you collapse and die? However they managed it, the roof had no sentries in the heat of the day, and Irma generally takes advantage of any opportunity.

Feet stomp and bowstrings swish as they release arrows. Metal clangs against metal and thwacks against wood and flesh. People shout and shriek in pain. Something—sounds like a body—thuds against the floor. I hope it's Irma and not one of the church people. If they manage to kill her, and my children are safe, my problems are over—unless the church people decide I'm a spy and should also be killed.

Heart pounding, I look around the storage room for a weapon. I settle for a length of cut wood.

"Stop!" Hannah shouts, but the sounds of battle continue. Children wail. The screams grow louder.

The fighting lasts a minute or two, then grows quiet except the sound of crying children.

"Where's Lucy?" Irma shouts. "Small woman, young, short brown hair, missing an ear."

My heart clenches. Irma's side won. I hope no one died, but ready myself for the slaughtered corpses of people who fed me and read to me.

I hear sobbing. "Let me help Magda," Hannah's raspy voice says. At least Hannah's still alive.

"Where's Lucy?" Irma repeats in a slow, deliberate voice.

"There," Hannah says.

The door unlatches and opens. Irma faces me, carrying a bloody machete and a shield made from an old oven door. Her deerskin clothes and a woven grass hat are soaking wet. Her vest is torn below the shoulder, the skin bloody beneath. The see-far glasses hang around her neck—she found my cache.

My skin tingles and turns cold. How will I explain hiding my belongings like that?

Breathing heavily, Irma looks me up and down. "You're uninjured?"

I nod, having no idea what to do now. "How? How'd you get here?"

"Followed your tracks, heard hammering, and found this place. Scouted and planned, kept to the river and a house basement during the day. River's not far from here and we brought water for cooling. Good thing we won—it was a one-way trip."

My fault. This attack was my fault. But at least Irma's not accusing me of anything. I point at her injury. "How deep is that?"

"It's nothing. Help Rod."

I step out and look around the basement. Bright red puddles cover the floor. A severed arm lies near the stairs, and a hand in the middle of the room. The arm is Nathan's—he lies on the concrete floor holding the stump of his right arm. Blood spurts between his fingers. A huge gash runs from the crown of his head to his ear, yellowish brain visible beneath the blood. The hand is Susanna's. She lies motionless with arrows in her chest and belly, a broken bow next to her.

The old man—Abraham—lies on his back, throat half-severed and still pumping out blood. There's an arrow in his groin, and his cutting pole has been sliced in two. Magda sits against the wall, impaled with arrows and moaning in pain.

Their God and their fortified church didn't protect them. Nothing can stop killers like Irma. The room spins and wobbles and I throw up foul-smelling bile, the only thing still in my stomach. It spatters the blood on the floor and mixes in.

Standing above the old man, Irma's oldest son, Rod, grips an arrow sticking through his upper right arm, and grimaces. A bloody machete lies at his feet, along with a big, blue-painted metal shield with two arrows halfway through.

"Don't try to pull it out," I warn him. He'll just make it worse.

Griff has an arrow-pierced shield similar to Rod's, and points a machete at Hannah. From the entrance, Bree aims a bow at the teenage girl named Phoebe. Bree and Tash have metal breastplates fastened to their deerskin vests. Tash sits on the stairs, her face flushed red from heat exhaustion.

Irma and Griff herd Hannah, Phoebe, and the four children together.

"Don't hurt them," I cry out.

"I knew you were a spy," Nathan gurgles at me. "How'd you signal...?" His voice rattles and his remaining arm drops. I watch the life disappear from his eyes.

Griff thrusts a spear deep into Magda's side. She coughs blood and slumps to the floor. People gasp and shout. "She was going to die anyway," he says.

"You don't know that," Hannah cries out. She turns to me with narrowed eyes that drip tears. "How could you do this to us?"

I want to say it's not my fault, but it is—I should have warned them. I should have never approached them. The room grows blurry and I want to hide beneath the straw in my room.

I turn away and wipe the tears from my eyes. My children aren't here. I ask Irma, "Where are Mary and Isaac? They're okay, right?"

"They're safe with Angelica. We'll get them when the sun goes down." She turns to the survivors and points her bloody machete toward the storage room. "Inside."

"Are you going to kill us too?" Phoebe asks.

"Not if you do what I say."

Irma and Griff herd the survivors into the storage room and latch the door. Irma glares at me. "I told you to help Rod."

Back to the way things were before. Probably forever. I take the string off Susanna's broken bow and tie it above Rod's arm puncture. I grip the lower arrow shaft and snap off the fletch end. Rod screams in pain. I don't care. I switch to the blade end and pull out the broken arrow. Blood dribbles from the entry and exit, but better than spurting.

"Wash it out and bandage it," I tell him. I'm not his mother.

Griff and Bree rustle through the church group's belongings. "They've got rabbits!" Bree shouts. "Hundreds of 'em!"

I pull off Tash's breastplate and clothes and give her water to drink. Irma pours water over her head.

We lead her to one of the beds. "You need to rest," Irma tells her.

Griff and Bree pass out raw tubers and pine seeds they've found. Everyone stuffs their mouths, not waiting to prepare a proper meal.

"The man I killed," Irma tells me, "thought you were a spy? But you don't want us to hurt them, even though they kept you prisoner?"

"They weren't going to kill me. They even fed me." I don't argue about the spy accusation—it wasn't true, but I'm under Irma's rule again.

"We found your weapons and the see-far glasses. Why did you hide them in the woods?"

I decide to tell the truth, sort of. "I went to talk to them and see if they had extra food."

"No one gives food away. That was stupid."

"I know." I've cost four people their lives. The type of people who feed strangers.

Across the room, Rod says, "I get the girl." His arm bandage leaks blood between the layered grass blades.

Griff scowls at him. "Why can't I have her? I killed more people than you."

Rod spits. "An old man and a dying woman."

I should be thankful they're not fixated on me anymore, but I'm disgusted beyond words. "Her name is Phoebe and she's a human being, not a piece of fish."

"Shut up everyone," Irma says. "Rod, Griff, you can share her. Try not to hurt her." She points at the dead bodies. "First, that's a month's worth of food if we don't let it spoil."

My belly squeezes inward in horror. Even Bree and Tash stare at Irma like they aren't sure they heard her right.

"It's no different than dressing a deer," she says.

I wonder if the children in the storage room can hear this, and if so, if they realize Irma intends to eat their parents.

"Humans aren't deer," I say.

"Meat is meat. There's rabbits here, but we can keep them alive till we need them."

"They breed them. There's no need to—"

"Rabbits are too lean without other food. And I'm tired of starving. I'm trying to keep you idiots alive, and all you can do is whine."

We've never eaten dead humans before. "These people survived fine on rabbits and grubs."

Irma frowns. Her tiny cupful of patience is almost gone. "I'm not throwing away good food, something as good as deer."

"What if it makes us sick?" I ask. "My mother told me eating deer brains can cause wasting disease."

"It's like any other meat. It won't make us sick as long as we cook it. But I know the saying not to eat animal brains." Her fists clench. "No more discussion. No matter what it takes, we'll never go hungry again."

I switch to another question, one that's more important. "What about the others? We're letting them go and moving on, right?"

"This is a good place to stay. Food, shelter, nearby water."

"At least let the others live," I plead. "We don't need to kill them."

Irma sighs. "I don't kill children. The old woman and the girl, they're no threat either, they didn't fight us."

Irma leaves me and kneels next to Nathan's mutilated body. He's closest and has the most muscle mass. She tells Bree to bring a bucket, then uses her carving knife to slice open the man's chest and belly. I turn away as she pulls out intestines and other organs and drops them in the bucket with a wet thump.

Irma's sons help her slice flesh off the body in thin strips. My stomach contracts like I'm going to throw up. I busy myself washing blood off the floor. Otherwise, the basement will begin to stink and fill with flies.

"Get over here, Lucy," Irma says.

I approach, expecting to be cursed at.

"You'd never survive on your own." She hands me the bucket of human organs.

It's surprisingly heavy. A bloody heart lies on top, with lungs just beneath.

"I saw the oven up there," she says. "Take Bree and start cooking before this spoils."

"The sun's out."

"Come back down while it's cooking." She takes off her wet hat and puts it on my head. "This will help."

Bree finds jars of salt and spices, and seasons the entrails while I start a fire in the oven.

"We'll cook the entrails for today and tomorrow," I tell Bree. "The meat, we'll lower the temperature and make jerky."

Then I break into uncontrollable sobs. These were people who fed me and gave me hope, and I'm helping cook them. Just yesterday, I was wondering how to learn from the mistakes of the Vanished Ones, how everyone could care about each other and heal the world. But now I'm back with a group that cares only about themselves. A group that will do anything to survive, no matter what. I'll never escape such a life, and was foolish to try it.

THAT NIGHT, IRMA OPENS the storage room door and tells the prisoners to come out. Their eyes are red-rimmed from crying. We've cleaned the basement, although we couldn't get all the blood stains off the floor.

"You can leave," Irma tells them. "Except you—" she points at Phoebe. "You stay."

Rod and Griff leer at the teenage girl, probably imagining tearing off her grass skirt and vest.

"We're not leaving without Phoebe," Hannah says.

Irma grips her machete.

I slip between the two. Enough blood has been spilled. "Let them all stay," I ask Irma. "They won't survive on their own."

"They're too many to watch," Irma says.

"They're children and an old woman. Please, like you spared Angelica."

Irma's face turns rigid as stone. "That was one mouth to feed, not six."

"They can help gather food," I say. "And breed the rabbits."

"We don't want to stay here," the sandy-skinned girl named Krista says.

Hannah glares at Irma and me. "You should leave, not us. This is our home, not yours."

Irma slaps Hannah hard in the face. "It's our home now."

Hannah puts a hand to her cheek, then grips her cross. "You are evil incarnate. You shall reap what you sow."

Irma whips her machete out of its scabbard. Rod and Griff do the same. "Out," Irma says, pointing the machete at Hannah. "I don't want to have to clean the floor again."

Rod leads the way up the stairs, while Irma and Griff prod Hannah and the four children forward.

We haven't cleaned upstairs yet, I remember. "Wait!" I shout, and hurry after them. I don't want the children to see our handiwork.

Irma and Griff ignore me. The prisoners spot the strips of drying jerky hanging from roof beams, and the pile of scraped bones and skulls that we planned to bury later tonight. Irma and her sons had been thorough except for the heads, from which they only removed the tongues, lips, and cheeks. From the nose up, they're still recognizable.

The children stare and shriek. Hannah drops to her knees. "Oh my Lord. This can't be."

I want to slink beneath the floor, even more ashamed than when we took the tower.

Irma tells everyone, "They were already dead, and we need the food. It's no different than eating a rabbit. Or dog."

The youngest child, who's barely past toddler age, drops to his knees before Magda's mutilated head and pees himself. "Mama! Mama!" He bawls and screams.

Bree and Tash are busy at the stove, preparing our night meal. Tash eyes the crying children, bites her lip, and starts to sniffle.

Irma motions to her sons, and the three drag the children and old woman to the front door. "Out!" Irma shouts. "I don't want to hurt anyone else! Don't come back!"

I find Hannah's Bible and run to her with it. "This is yours. What else do you need?"

Eyes narrowed and teeth clenched, she holds up a hand, refusing to accept it. "We were happy before you arrived." She spits out the words. "Our children will never recover from what you've done, and you've stolen our shelter and food—everything we need to survive. Think about that when you look your own children in the eyes."

She's right. I still have nightmares about my mother being slaughtered, and what we did was worse. Tears blur my vision.

"Let Phoebe join us," Hannah continues. "She doesn't deserve whatever you fiends have planned for her." Her eyes narrow with anger. "Then leave and never return." She turns and leads the children into the battered forest.

Knowing Irma and her sons, neither of those will happen today. But maybe eventually. I'll work on it once I'm with Mary and Isaac again—they're my main priority. And as soon as I can, I'll run far away, settle with my children and Angelica along a river with fish, in a big city of the Vanished Ones.

We'll try to live like the church people instead of wandering cannibals.

I put the rejected Bible in my carry bag and return to Irma. "I need my children."

The hardness has disappeared from her eyes. "I'll take you after we eat."

I don't want my children to know what we did. I address Irma's sons and daughters. "Please bury the bones and heads before we come back. And if my children ask about the jerky, say we killed a deer."

Irma tells them, "Do it."

IRMA LEADS ME TO A ruined house with a mostly-intact basement. Mary runs to me and I lift her into the air.

"I'm sorry I was gone so long," I say. "It'll never happen again." I cover her cheeks with kisses and put her down, then give her a final squeeze. I appreciate her more than ever now.

Angelica passes Isaac to me. "We all missed you, chera."

I rock Isaac in my arms and he smiles. His tiny hands reach toward my chest so I untie my deerskin shirt and breast feed him. I've had plenty of food the past few days and give him all the milk he wants.

We head back to the church. As we near, I smell smoke. Irma sniffs the air and starts running.

I pass Isaac to Angelica and pick up Mary. "Hurry," I tell Angelica, and we move as fast as we can. We lose sight of Irma, but I know the way.

The smoke grows stronger as we rush forward. It's not just wood burning—I smell burning meat too. An orange glow appears through the trees. A girl shrieks in pain.

We reach the clearing. The church roof and interior are consumed in writhing flames that crackle the wood and reach high into the sky, belching greasy gray smoke toward the stars. Our food and supplies are in there. And all those books. Only the Bible in my carry bag remains, and the plant book from the estuario tower.

Rod and Griff are sitting on the grass outside, Rod with a hand to his neck and Griff holding his belly and groaning. Bree stares at the burning building as Irma shouts, "Tash! Tash!"

Sparks drift into the dry grass around the church and ignite more fires. Smoke stings my eyes and Isaac begins to wail. Beyond the clearing, flames erupt among the trees all around us, further away than the drifting sparks. Mary clings to me, her face terrified.

Where to go? The old road passing the church is bordered by pine trees full of flammable sap. It's been a month since the big storm, everything is bone dry, and there's downed wood and needles everywhere. The fires around us spread fast and converge, flames swirling and roaring in the heat, leaping up tree after tree and engulfing them like torches. We're trapped.

The graveyard is the only refuge. Hundreds of closely-spaced gravestones. About half the graves are covered by low concrete slabs.

"There," I tell Angelica, pointing. We dodge patches of burning grass and look for a safe spot.

I pick a concrete grave surrounded by other slabs and as far from trees as possible. We huddle on top. Mary and Isaac cry and I hold them. Angelica whimpers. Smoke enters my nose and stings my eyes.

Tash's screaming stops. Irma keeps shouting her name.

The grass fires invade the graveyard. Past the clearing, the entire forest blazes bright orange. Irma leads Bree, Rod, and Griff around to the far side of the church.

The flames approach. We're too close to the burning trees, which throw off waves of heat. If they start to fall... "Get ready to move," I say. I crouch down and tell Mary, "Climb on my back." I hold Isaac in my arms and stand with Mary clinging to my neck. I tell Angelica, "Follow me."

If we jump over the advancing grass fire, which is less dangerous than the forest fire, we can reach the area that's already burned. It won't burn again any time soon.

When the fire reaches our slab, flames rising from the dry grass, I bend my legs and jump for the adjacent slab with every bit of energy I have. With Mary clinging to my neck and Isaac in my arms, my leap is clumsy. I feel sharp pain in my feet and ankles, and when we land on the neighboring slab, I lose my balance and tumble to the ground, throwing up a cloud of ash. But we're on the other side of the flames. My moccasins and pants are charred, but weren't exposed long enough to catch fire.

"I can't do it," Angelica says.

"You have to."

She grits her teeth and sort of jumps—it's more of a step and a hop. Flames lick against her moccasins and pants, and she screams in pain. She stumbles onto our slab, clothes blackened but not alight. "You could have helped."

"My hands were full. Are you alright?"

She doesn't answer, but her deerskins didn't catch fire, so she should be fine.

From the other side of the church, Irma screams, "Lucy! We need you!"

Most of the grass has burned already. We follow the blackened ground around the still-flaming church. The moon and stars are obscured by smoke, but the fires cast plenty of light.

Irma, Bree, Rod, and Griff are covered in soot. Rod and Griff's clothes are soaked with blood.

Irma beckons me over. "Rod and Griff have been stabbed. Can you help them?"

I pass Isaac to Angelica. "What happened?"

Neither boy answers. Rod is holding a blood-drenched rabbit skin against his throat.

"That Phoebe girl," Irma says. "She stabbed them, then she set the church on fire."

"How?"

Irma glares at her sons. "I asked the same thing."

"She had a knife," Griff says. He winces in pain. "Hidden in the straw. She cut Rod's neck, then stabbed me in the belly."

Irma raises her fist, but doesn't strike them like they deserve. "The two of you couldn't control one girl?"

Still holding the rabbit skin against his throat, Rod points at his bandaged arm.

"Let me guess," I tell Irma's sons. "You tried to rape Phoebe and weren't expecting her to fight back."

They just glare at me, meaning the answer is yes.

"Just help them," Irma asks me. Her mouth trembles with distress. "Tash didn't make it out. My little flower."

I've never seen Irma like this, even after Thal died. She must have been more attached to her youngest than I thought.

"Where's the medical bag?" I ask.

Irma points to the burning church. The roof collapses as we watch, sending up an explosion of sparks. "Medical bag, shields, most of our weapons... everything's in there."

'You shall reap what you sow,' I remember Hannah saying. The simultaneous fires erupting all around us—Phoebe couldn't have done that by herself. Hannah and the children must have helped, wreaking vengeance for the harm we caused them.

We're bad people, I realize. Like the painted killers who slaughtered my mother and nearly everyone else I knew. We're no different. We deserve this punishment. Myself included.

I put aside the thoughts and examine Rod. The blade sliced across his neck, spilling a lot of blood, but the wound is superficial, well short of the main arteries and veins. I cut off one of his shirt sleeves and tie it around his neck, tossing away the bloody rabbit skin. "You'll live."

Griff is another matter. The knife punctured his intestines. With the needle and thread in the medical bag, maybe I could fix him, but without it, I can't. And there's no plant fiber within sight to weave more thread—everything's burnt.

"Keep pressing your tunic against the wound," I tell him. At least that might slow the bleeding.

I don't really care if he dies. We might all die now, and it's his and Rod's fault. Irma's too.

Around us, the forest fires continue to rage. The sky is obscured by smoke and I'm not sure what time it is. "We need to find shelter," I tell Irma.

She points west toward the river. "Fire's blocking the way."

A thought occurs. It's distasteful, but our only option. We could dig up some of the graves and lie in the coffins until nightfall again. Not all the graves are covered with concrete slabs. And the church group had shovels among their tools.

I quietly ask Griff if he followed our instructions about burying the remains of the people we cooked.

He nods. "Me and Rod."

"Where are the shovels?"

"By the hole."

I tell Irma my plan. She agrees.

We pick up the shovels and start digging up two of the more recent graves that aren't sealed: Emma Swan, 2021-2075, and Kaitlin Swan, 2050-2075. The years of their birth and death. No one I've met keeps track of years anymore, so I have no idea when that was. But the stone etchings are still easily readable through the circles of lichen. Like everything from the Vanished World, it seems so close, like I could reach out and bring it all back.

The soil is loose, and digging is easier than it would be elsewhere. Bree and Rod help, taking over when I get too tired. Angelica helps also, while Mary takes care of Isaac.

We force open the metal caskets with our shovels, revealing waxy yellow skeletons and tattered cloth, most of it whitish. The skeletons disintegrate when we try to remove them.

The sky is still obscured by smoke, but it's getting lighter to the east. There's no way eight people will fit in two graves, even if we are all shorter than the skeletons.

"We need to dig more," I say, "and hurry."

"Bree, Angelica," Irma orders, "clean out those caskets."

Irma, Rod, and I dig up two more graves. My arms and back ache, and I struggle to summon enough energy to continue. Even Irma sweats and breathes heavily.

We finally finish. Above the horizon, the sun glows orange-red through the smoke and haze, like a bloody moon angry at the world.

Rod and Griff share the far casket, Irma and Bree share one, and Angelica gets one to herself. I lie with Mary and Isaac in a now-bare metal box. They don't take up much space and can barely keep their eyes open. I close the lid of the casket, propping open an air gap with my shovel. It's hot inside, but the casket is shaded and in contact with the deep earth, and noticeably cooler than the surface. I'm so exhausted, I fall asleep almost immediately.

WHEN NIGHT FALLS, I push open the lid of my casket and crawl out of my grave. Mary passes Isaac to me, then I pull Mary out.

Only blackened, windowless walls remain of the church, wisps of white smoke still curling from the wreckage within. The fires have finished consuming the forest around us, but continue to march across the storm-battered landscape. The eastern and southern horizons glow orange, and the stars are obscured by smoke.

Irma, Bree, Angelica, and Rod emerge from their graves too. But not Griff.

"Griff's dead," Rod says in a croaking voice.

Irma's jaw drops. She slips into his grave. I hear muttering, but nothing I can make out.

She climbs out and stomps toward me. "You were supposed to save him!"

"Our medical supplies burned, and all the plants we could make more from."

She glares at me, but doesn't raise her fists. Maybe she realizes there wasn't anything I could do, and Griff brought his death upon himself.

I'm starving, but there's nothing to eat whatsoever. All around us, the land has turned to charcoal and ash. We're also nearly out of water.

My eyes rest on the open grave that Rod climbed out of. *No matter what it takes, we'll never go hungry again*, Irma told me yesterday. If I want my children to live, I have to think that way too.

"Irma," I tell her quietly, "we should cook Griff before the meat spoils."

Her eyes widen. She doesn't answer for a while, then she nods.

I instruct Angelica and Bree to take my children to the other side of the burned church. I loan Bree my bow and machete for defense—she lost everything in the fire.

When they're out of sight, I cut open Griff's body and pull out the organs. The intestines have already spoiled, so I toss those into his open casket. Rod builds a stone oven while Irma and I dismember the body and cut the meat off in thin strips. We cut the organs into small pieces so they'll cook fast and be unrecognizable.

We search the church wreckage and find some blades with charred handles. We also recover the iron cauldron. There's no sign of Tash—probably burnt to bones and buried beneath fragments of collapsed roof and floor.

I boil the organ pieces, then lower the heat and begin drying the meat in the stone oven. Irma tosses the bones into the casket and shuts the lid. When we're ready to eat, she calls Angelica and the children back.

"This is awful," Mary complains about her liver chunks.

"Sorry," I say. It's extremely nutritious, but she's right about the strong metallic taste and the squishy texture. "We lost all our spices."

Bree refuses to eat—she knows where the food came from. Irma tells her, "I'm not losing another child. Eat or I'll shove it down your throat."

Bree takes a bite of kidney, chews, then gags and spits it out.

I figure when she gets hungry enough, she'll change her mind.

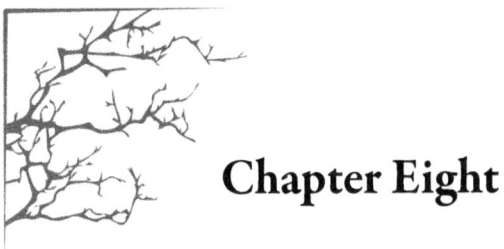

Chapter Eight

Because it took all night to search the ruins and prepare the jerky, we have to spend another day in the graves. We unearth a new casket for Rod, which he gets to himself.

We climb out the next night and trek west through the scorched wasteland. The ground is still hot and smoldering in places. But we have no choice—we've run out of water. As for food, the jerky will last four days, I estimate. I carry Isaac on my back, and Irma lets Mary sit on her shoulders. Even walking carefully, my feet grow warm through the moccasins.

My stomach drops when we reach the river. It's black with ash and choked with debris. Even if we boil it, the water could poison us.

Irma grinds her teeth, probably thinking the same thing. "We had shelter and food, now we have nothing. And Tash and Griff are dead." Her face snarls with anger. "I'll tear that girl apart if we find her."

I don't respond. We deserved what happened. "We need water. We have to keep going."

We follow the river upstream and cross where it's shallow. Nobody speaks. We take a narrow, pitted road to the continuation of the wide roadway that brought us here. The splintered pine forest hasn't burned here, not recently anyway.

I feel like someone's following us, but when I turn, no one's there.

"You shall reap what you sow," Hannah's voice echoes in my ears. "You are evil incarnate."

I could have warned her group, but didn't. Just like the tower group. Violent death follows my every footstep. It's like Irma and her children and me were 'fected by the painted-face monsters who slaughtered the rest of our clan, then we turned into monsters ourselves.

As the still-smoky eastern horizon turns dull orange, we come to a stream and drink at last. Then we search for a place to hide from the daylight.

WE FINALLY EXIT THE region of storm damage and enter a gently rolling landscape of pines and oaks. It looks like it rains more here than at the estuario—the understory has all kinds of plants. We even find crabapple trees. Their fruit is mouth-wincing tart when eaten raw, but we cook them with acorns, tubers, and insects. It's the best meal I've had since leaving the church.

Rod and Bree make new bows, and spears that double as walking sticks. Mary and I collect medicinal and spice plants, and begin weaving more carry bags.

Our third night on the wide road, I spot two metal towers rising high above the tree canopy, dark against the starlit sky. I ask Irma, "Can I borrow the see-far glasses?"

"Why?"

I point to the taller of the two towers. "We could see a long way from up there."

Irma hands me the glasses. The towers are open frames of metal beams with weird attachments on the sides and top. I've seen these before, during my childhood journey away from the mountains, but usually they're collapsed or broken in two.

I return the glasses and Irma looks too. "You want to climb that?"

I'm not sure, now that she asks. "If it's safe. But if it's still standing, it must be pretty sturdy." Unless it's because we're far from the coast now—the storms seem to be worse there.

Irma seems to read my mind yet again. "This area might work. No giant storms, no big wildfires. And no other groups so far."

"I'll look for signs of food, water, and shelter," I say.

And cooking fires, I think. Our encounters with other groups always end badly, but if I find another friendly group, I'll kill Irma and Rod in their sleep. Hack off their heads with my machete. If I can bring myself to do it.

THE METAL-FRAME TOWERS are located among sprawling single-story buildings, most with collapsed roofs. The towers look even taller close-up, like I could touch the stars from the top. The bigger one has four sides and the smaller has three.

I hang the see-far glasses around my neck and hand my carry bag, water flask, and weapons to Mary and Angelica. I start climbing the ladder up the taller tower. The metal is rusty in spots, especially around the bolts. I focus on one step at a time, raising a hand, raising a foot, raising the other hand, raising the other foot, over and over.

I'm above treetop level when a rung breaks off beneath my foot. I seize in terror. The rung falls with a clatter, leaving me hanging by the arms, feet dangling in the air, hard concrete at the bottom. I might die. I don't want to die!

I don't have big arm muscles like Thal did, but I've spent years carrying Mary and Isaac, and I hold on tight. I lower myself down to the rung below, which held my weight earlier. My heart hammers against my chest.

The tower has diagonal rods that help hold it together. I pause to catch my breath, then head back up, putting my feet on the diagonals to pass the ladder gap. From here, I test each rung carefully. Two more break on the way up, but I'm ready this time and don't panic.

I finally reach the top. It's windy up here. The eastern sky is brightening. The light will make my climb down easier, but I'll have to hurry before it gets too hot.

I look down for the first time and nearly pee myself. Three tiny figures wait far below—Angelica and my two children. This was a stupid idea.

I hook my arms and feet around the sides of the ladder, then scan the horizon. To the north, a dome of bare rock rises high above the expanse of trees. The west is even more interesting. Our wide road leads to a line of tall buildings, each one far bigger than any previous remnant of the Vanished World I've seen. It must have been their main city, full of treasures beyond imagining.

There might be people there, too. If so, I hope they are more like the church people than Irma or the painted-face murderers in the mountains. If there are lots of them, and they have access to books and artifacts, my children will have another chance at a good life.

I squeeze my body against as many metal bars as possible, hoping I won't lose my balance, and look through the see-far glasses. Except the forest fires far to the east, I don't see any smoke. In the direction of the tall buildings, I see more metal towers like the one I'm on. The tall buildings vary in height and width. Some have triangular roofs. One is round, like a giant tree trunk. I don't see any rivers or streams, but they could be hidden by trees.

I look down again and think about waving, but I'm too afraid of falling. I begin the long climb down.

I'M EXHAUSTED WHEN my feet finally reach solid ground. But my head swirls with relief and happiness. I'm alive. I climbed all the way up that tower and back down again.

Everyone's there to greet me. Their water flasks are full and their carry bags bulge with food. Bree holds up a dead squirrel, the first one I've seen in years. "Look what I shot! We got acorns and tree bark too."

"What did you find?" Irma asks me.

I tell everyone about the big city to the west. "The buildings are so big, you wouldn't even notice the estuario tower. And I didn't see any cooking fires." My skin tingles with all the possibilities. "A place that big will have a river too."

"Did you see one?"

"Too far away—we have to get closer."

We shelter in one of the few intact nearby buildings, which has a cavernous interior and high ceiling that's collapsed in places. Rows of dusty metal racks extend from wall to wall, some piled with junk.

"No basements nearby," Irma says. "But it's a little cooler in here."

We prepare our daytime meal. While Bree and Angelica cook, Irma and Rod make traps to catch mice and rats. Bree tells me I deserve a break, so I explore the metal racks with Mary.

Most of the racks are empty, but some contain rodent-chewed remnants of boxes. Within them are moldy clothes and books that fall apart when I touch them, flakes and melted lumps of colored plastic, and corroded pieces of metal. But we find some treasures that are still intact—pots and pans, knives and forks, hammers and nails, and glass bottles. I find a plastic doll and give it to Mary. It's a thin light-skinned woman with long blonde hair and pink clothes.

The doll's clothes disintegrate as Mary examines it. "Is this what the Vanished Ones looked like?" she asks.

"I doubt their legs were that long," I say. Other than that, I have no idea.

I find leather carry bags in some of the tattered boxes, most coated with mold. Two, still wrapped in plastic, are sturdy. I wipe the bags clean and fill them with cookware and other supplies. We return to the others.

"Look what we found!" Mary says.

Everyone congratulates her. I hug her and kiss the top of her head.

This building seems like the perfect home, but the temperature becomes nearly unbearable as the sun rises. If the ceiling wasn't so high, we'd probably overheat. But sleep is impossible.

WELL AFTER SUNSET, Irma and Rod check their traps. They bring back a bag of dead mice and rats to supplement the last of our tree bark and Griff jerky. Then we continue west on the wide road, past more pines and oaks. I'm tired and groggy.

The road crosses two dried-up creeks, but no rivers. After more walking, we pass beneath two dirty green signs fastened to a metal overhang. The signs have white-lettered place names, which mean nothing to me, and the number '285' inside a red and blue half-circle.

Below the signs, a wide spiral is chiseled into the road surface, its depth and edges uneven. It doesn't look like a Vanished World creation, but must have taken days to create. I wonder how old it is, who made it, and what it means. Are there people living here? If so, what are they like? Friendly or dangerous? Have they learned the secrets of the Vanished Ones? Or are they long gone, like most people?

Past an intersection with another wide road, we find a narrow creek with slow-moving water. We leave the road and fill our flasks and bottles.

"Can we stay here?" Mary asks me. "I'm tired of walking."

"What do you think?" I ask Irma. "Look for the nearest basement?"

Irma points north. "Sunrise is hours away. We need food too."

We follow the creek and search for signs of game. I don't see any animal tracks, or any fish bigger than a minnow, but the water is shallow and the banks are overgrown with weeds and vines. It's too dark beneath the thick tree canopy, anyway.

Mary trips over something and falls. I rush over and help her up. "Are you alright?"

She nods, then looks down and inhales sharply. A mud-spattered human skull lies by her feet, missing its jawbone and teeth.

"It's just a skull," I tell my daughter.

"I don't like this place," she says.

"Me either. It's too dark to see."

Irma waves her arm and leads us out of the stream valley. We take a narrow, broken road that follows the creek. As we walk, we watch our surroundings for movement or cooking fires, and listen for breaking twigs or rustling leaves.

Between the trees, old roads and ruined houses are everywhere. Most of the houses look burnt. Still no sign of game, but we find unripe persimmons, and gather the ones within reach. Then we get lucky—peach trees with ripe fruit on their upper branches! Bree is light, and clambers up the nearest tree. She breaks off a side branch, strips off the leaves, and uses it to knock down the peaches.

They're juicy and delicious. But as we stuff our stomachs, I wonder who or what picked the fruit from the lower branches.

I search for footsteps, but none remain since the last time it rained.

The sky brightens. We find a three-story brick building that's still intact except for broken windows and smashed-in doors. It doesn't have a basement, but the bottom floor rests against a hillside covered by sheets of rusting metal. It will have to do.

The tattered, dusty carpeting inside is splattered red-brown. A lot of blood was spilled here. Spirals, like the one we saw entering the city, are traced in stale blood on the walls. My breath catches and I find myself backing away. Mary grips my right hand, nails digging into my palm.

"What do you think happened here?" Rod asks his mother.

"A fight that's long over," Irma says.

"Thal would say this place is cursed," Angelica says. "Can we leave?"

I want to leave too, but the sun's over the horizon. And we still haven't seen other people, only past signs. "We'll leave as soon as night falls," I tell her, then meet Irma's eyes.

She nods. "It'll be coolest in the back."

We follow a hallway to the furthest rooms—thankfully no blood there—and set up a guard rotation.

"We should return to the estuario," I say. Killers live in this city.

Angelica and Mary voice their agreement. "I don't like this place," Mary says.

Irma shakes her head. "Everything's burned that direction. How would we survive the journey? And we can't live in the tower without boats."

THE NEXT NIGHT, WE return to the peach trees and gather the rest of the fruit. Mary and I return to the stream and collect more water, which will have to be boiled. I also find a tangle of blackberry bushes. Like the peaches, most of the fruit has been picked. But we search carefully and find a lot of ripe berries still on the branches.

Mary eats whatever she finds. "Peaches and berries! No more rat meat!"

None of us want to sleep in the building with the blood stains again, so we take a narrow road north. We find burned remnants of houses among the trees, but none have intact basements. The road widens, then ends at a collapsed bridge. Below the bridge are rusty train rails—lots of them. Like other train roads I've seen, the paired metal strips stretch beyond sight in either direction, with age-cracked wooden beams and weed-covered gravel beneath. Rust-streaked old trains rest on the furthest rails, covered with vines.

"Train roads often lead to tunnels," Irma says.

It's as good an idea as any. The eastern sky is beginning to lighten. We scramble down to the tracks and follow them west. After maybe ten minutes of walking, the tracks curve slightly to the right. Ahead are two tunnel entrances, mouths of darkness in a concrete wall.

Irma turns to us with a rare smile on her face. "Perfect."

I draw my machete in case we aren't the only ones who think that. Like whoever took the easy-to-reach peaches and whoever spilled blood in the brick building. Irma and her children pull out weapons too.

Irma leads us into the tunnel. The air is definitely cooler inside.

"Stop!" she says a minute later. She points at a circle of viciously toothed metal with a pressure plate in the middle. An old animal trap. It's chained to one of the train rails.

I examine the trap. Like the rails, it's rusty, and coated with a fine layer of dust. It's obviously been here a while. But if it still works, the teeth would punch right through clothes and flesh, and probably break the ankle.

We proceed carefully, and stop before the tunnel gets too dark to see. Irma starts a fire and we cook our day meal. Further down the tunnel, barely illuminated by our cooking fire, I spot another trap.

What if Mary steps in one of these traps? The thought makes me shiver. I take a piece of firewood to this other trap.

"What you are doing?" Irma shouts behind me.

"Another trap. We should spring them all so it's safe to walk around."

"Leave them," she says. "They're a good defense if we know where they are."

That's stupid, I think. We should spring all the tunnel traps and move them closer to the entrance. Maybe we'll even catch a deer if there are any.

My lips form a smile. I have a better idea. Find out where all the traps are, but don't tell Irma or her children. Maybe even move some of them.

No matter what it takes. Tomorrow night I'll escape.

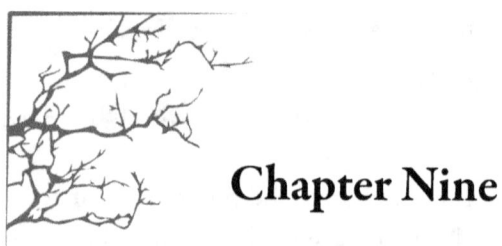

Chapter Nine

We wake when night falls. The fire is dead—not even smoldering—and it's so dark, I can't even see my hands.

During my time on watch—which I'd shared with Bree—I'd lit a pine sap torch and walked far into the tunnel. A whole cluster of traps lay just beyond the light of our cooking fire. Frightening. After that, nothing—at least as far as I'd dared to go. Bree had asked me if I saw anything. I'd lied and said no, it was all clear.

A spark flashes in the darkness, accompanied by the *chih* of steel against flint. Two more strikes and Irma's rekindled our fire. She's good at that, I have to admit.

I refill my torch with pine sap, stuffing it between the splits I'd cut on the top end. I'll need it to escape. As we boil drinking water and prepare our night meal, I pull Angelica aside and whisper, "There's more traps inside. Don't tell anyone else."

"Why not?" she whispers back.

"We're leaving Irma and Rod tonight."

Angelica bites her lip. "Vea? Why?"

"A thousand reasons why. I don't want to be around killers and rapists anymore."

She's quiet for a while, then says, "You go. I can't run."

I start to argue, but she's right. She'll slow me down. It will be hard enough to escape with Isaac and Mary.

"I won't tell anyone," she says.

Mary screams. It echoes off the walls and sends chills up my spine. She's pointing at the tunnel entrance. Isaac starts to cry.

Human-shaped figures are approaching the entrance, silent shadows in the moonlight. I count eight. I place Isaac in my back sling in case I have to run. We scramble for our bows.

The figures enter the tunnel. Our fire light reveals details. Their faces and arms are darkened to blend in with the night, they carry bows and long knives, and wear black plastic helmets and metal plates painted with spirals, misshapen eyes, and jagged teeth. The spirals look like the ones we saw painted in blood the night before.

My hands shake—they're not like the church people, they're like the striped-faced monsters who slaughtered my mother. We back away from the fire so we're harder to see.

The figures unleash a volley of arrows. Rod is hit in the thigh, and Bree in the left shoulder.

Irma yells "Go fuck yourselves!" and shoots back. So do Rod and I.

Rod misses. My arrow bounces off a breastplate. But Irma's pierces an attacker's throat. The figure gurgles and drops its bow.

"You're messing with the wrong people!" Irma shouts.

We shoot at each other again. Heart racing, I aim for the legs, which are unprotected.

An arrow splits Rod's knuckles. He screeches in pain. Irma is hit in the forehead, but it glances off to the right, leaving a stream of blood.

My shot misses—the targets are moving—and the other arrows bounce off armor.

I know a losing battle when I see it. And this is my chance to be free of Irma forever. I shoulder my bow and light my torch. Then I kick the cooking fire apart, the heat burning my toes through the moccasin, but not bad enough to slow me.

I grab Mary by the hand and start running down the tunnel. Arrows clatter against the concrete behind me. From my back sling, Isaac cries.

"Run, Angelica!" I shout behind my shoulder. I don't want her to die, but I can't wait for her—she's too slow.

Behind me, Irma screams, "Come back, you coward!"

Go fuck yourself, Irma, I think as I run. You deserve to die. But I'm not dying with you. I don't want Mary and Isaac to die. I just need you and your children to keep the attackers busy so I can escape.

I hear footsteps behind me. Someone else is running, maybe more than one person. I dodge between the animal traps, guiding Mary around them too.

The shouts, clatters, and thunks of battle echo behind me. Someone wheezes and gurgles, "I tried. Go fuck yourself, world." It's Irma's voice.

Then a clank and crunch, followed by a girl's shriek. Someone must have stepped in a trap. The high pitch sounds like Bree. I hope it wasn't Angelica.

At least it wasn't me. I keep running and don't look back.

"I can't keep up," Mary complains.

I'm practically dragging her. But I can't carry both her and Isaac, especially if I have to light the way. "Try. You have to try." I slow to a rate I think she can manage.

A slightly brighter square appears ahead. It must be the tunnel exit. What if there are enemies on that side too? I stop to quiet Isaac, then tell Mary, "We have to be careful."

I glance behind me and see nothing but darkness. I hear distant noises, but they're too muffled to make out.

I lead Mary toward the exit, walking fast instead of running. It's still too dark to put out the torch—there might be more traps.

I hear echoing footsteps ahead. My heart skips a beat and I stop.

Outlined by the exit, dark figures are advancing toward me. I can't tell how many there are. Mary spots them too and digs nails into my palm. There's nowhere to go, no other exit from this tunnel. And no place to hide.

What do I do? Fight? One against many? Run back the way we came and face the first group of enemies?

There is no solution. It's over. I hurl my torch as far as I can toward the shadows. It flies end over end, trailing sparks, and crashes between the train rails. The pine pitch burns bright, lighting the advancing figures. At least six bow-carrying men and women with darkened faces, black helmets, and frightening armor. The bearded man in front wears a breastplate painted with a large bloodshot eye emitting black flames.

I call out, "I'm just a mother with a child and a baby. I don't want to fight you."

The bearded man in front laughs, a wheezing hammer-like sound that chills my spine. The figures continue forward.

I think about praying to the spirits like Angelica used to, but what good did it do her? I tell Mary and Isaac, "You'll be fine. Healthy children are too valuable to kill."

Especially children from another group. My father had told me tales of inbred families in other mountain valleys with severe deformities and an inability to speak.

The burning pitch reveals more details. The others wear necklaces of fingers and toes and backbones. Their eyes are wild, like they're crazy, not even really human.

Heart pounding, I put out my palms, showing I'm not holding weapons. "I'm sorry if we intruded on your territory." I'm not sure this is their territory, but someone placed those traps in the tunnel—possibly to catch humans like us. "I just want to leave. I'll go far away."

I hold Mary's hand and resume walking toward the exit.

"Alive," the man in front growls. The wild-eyed people rush me, hit me, knock me down, grip my arms and legs. They take my carry bag and weapons, and pull Isaac and Mary away.

"No!" My arms and legs thrash, almost on their own. I'm hit or kicked in the head so hard, I see stars like the twinkling dots that passed above our tower every night, back where we were safe and well-fed and learning how to read and hoping to bring back the wonders of the Vanished World.

WHEN I REGAIN MY SENSES, I'm being hauled out of the tunnel. My wrists and ankles are bound, tight enough that I can't move them. Mary and Isaac are bawling as loud as I've ever heard them.

I whip my head that direction. Two of my attackers lift Mary and drop her into a big blue plastic container with wheels on the bottom. Another, with paint-darkened female features and jagged red lines painted on her helmet and breastplate, places Isaac into Mary's hands. "Hold baby," she tells Mary. "You stay in bin."

"Don't hurt them!" I shout.

The bearded man with the black-flaming eye on his breastplate slaps me hard across the face. "Shut mouth." I see stars again, followed by pain.

Two pick me up and dump me into a metal-frame cart with mismatched wheels and a push bar. It's one of several.

Six grim-faced men and women emerge from the tunnel. I recognize the spirals, eyes, and teeth painted on their armor—they're the ones who attacked from the other side. A husky man behind Angelica grips her by the wrists and pushes her forward. Angelica looks uninjured, but her face is slack, as if she's beyond emotion or thought. Her captor has finger bones braided in his beard, and a seven-headed lizard-creature is painted on his breastplate.

The other five drag motionless bodies—Irma, Rod, Bree, and two of their own. Irma's dead at last. She'd be proud of herself, though, killing two of the enemy.

The big man with the finger bones in his beard picks up Angelica and plops her in a metal cart like mine. He waves Eye-Flames over. They talk quietly, then bark out orders.

Some of the crazies stand watch. The rest gut and bleed the bodies, dumping the entrails into metal buckets and collecting the blood in glass jars. They place the buckets and jars in one cart, and dump the bodies in the others.

A man pushes my cart along the pitted concrete adjacent to the train rails. The cart rattles and shakes. Just ahead of me, the woman painted with jagged red lines pushes the tall blue container with Mary and Isaac. I hear more carts behind me.

We travel a short distance beneath the open sky, then enter another tunnel. My captors don't light torches—they can either see in the dark or know the tunnels by feel and sound. No one talks.

After a while, we emerge from the tunnel. Concrete walls rise on either side, so I can't tell where we are. But by the position of the stars, we're heading west.

Tall buildings come into view—the ones I saw from the metal frame tower, only much closer. A shorter building, almost directly ahead, looks older, and is topped by a golden dome. Is that where they're taking us? Is it the center of the Vanished World?

Instead, the tracks curve to the right and enter a large blocky building with broken windows. We follow the tracks through the building and continue onward, surrounded by concrete walls and roofs. We stop inside a long tiled room, faintly lit from the outside, with dusty blue signs that read 'Five Points.' It's cool in here, like the tunnels.

More people greet us. Their faces aren't painted black and they aren't wearing helmets. They carry spears and machetes, though, and stare at me with hungry eyes.

The big man with bones in his beard and the painted seven-headed lizard seems to be in charge, with Eye-Flames second in command. They shout orders and the others tip over most of the carts, including mine. My elbow and head bang against the metal bars.

Dirty hands drag me out of the tipped cart. Others dump out Mary and Isaac out of the blue container. Their cries are terrifying.

Wrists and ankles still tied, I inchworm toward my children. Someone kicks me hard in the ribs and I collapse in pain. I start to say something but know it won't help.

Unpainted people strip the bodies, divide their belongings, and carry the naked, bloody corpses up solid metal stairs, along with the buckets of entrails.

Bone-Beard approaches me with a large sharp knife. He grins, exposing brown and yellow teeth, and points his knife at my ear stump. "Someone try eat you already."

My skin turns cold. They're going to eat the dead, then they'll eat me. And probably Angelica. And my children?

"Let us join you," I say. Children are valuable and so are fertile women in good health, especially ones with lots of skills like me. "I'm a healer."

Bone-Beard looks me up and down. He cuts the rope around my ankles and points to another set of metal stairs, leading down. "This way." His breath smells rotten.

"Not without my children." My eyes meet Mary's and then I run for her and Isaac, so quickly, no one can stop me. I kneel with them and wish my wrists weren't bound so I could hold them, somehow protect them.

Filthy hands grip me, grip my children. A sharp blade presses against my neck. "You do what we say or all die."

"Let us join you," I repeat, even though the thought disgusts me. Irma was also a killer, but at least she was kin and I understood her. These people can't even speak properly—maybe two generations away from grunting. I can run away though, when they aren't watching.

Bone-Beard removes his knife from my throat and yanks me up by the armpits. Another joins him and points a spear at me. I stand quietly. They said earlier if I followed orders, they wouldn't kill us. That's all I care about.

I spot Angelica. Eye-Flames presses a grimy hand against her bulging belly. "Good," he says. "Still alive."

"Move," the man with the spear tells me, and pokes me with the point.

Bone-Beard leads and I follow. We take the stairs down to another level, dimly lit by wood fires. The rusty stairs are grooved, with points at the end as if to slice your ankles if you aren't careful.

The air is even cooler at the bottom, but reeks of old smoke. Two more train roads run through the long space and disappear into tunnels in either direction. I don't see many people, but bedding and belongings cover much of the concrete floor. This must be where most of these people sleep during the day. The walls are painted with spirals and wild eyes and screaming mouths and misshapen figures with horns. The shifting orange light from the wood fires makes the wall pictures look alive.

"Move," Bone-Beard commands. He leads us forward. Out of the flickering gloom appears a shape my mind can't seem to process.

"Stop."

Details flood in. Before us, brown-tinged human bones spiral around a horrific statue propped against a wide rectangular column and held together with plastic cords and sheets of thick wire. The statue resembles a huge upright lizard constructed from red-painted pelvises and rib cages, with a coiled tail made from thigh bones. The lizard has seven heads, each a grinning human skull painted a different color, and seven arms, each holding a green-tinged trumpet. At the base of the lizard are seven skeletal feet, before which rest seven wooden bowls, each half-filled with rancid-smelling blood.

I freeze in place, like a mouse trapped in a corner. The seven-headed monster stares at me with empty sockets that blink in the firelight. The room loses focus and spins around me.

"Kneel," Bone-Beard commands. Something sharp jabs me in the back. The man with the spear.

I obey.

The statue must have taken a lot of effort to construct. It's worse in its repulsive artistry than my worst nightmares, the ones about the striped-faced hill people killing my mother. The largest group of people I've ever encountered, in the greatest stronghold of the Vanished Ones I've seen, are insane beyond words.

I hear footsteps on the metal stairs. Eye-Flames and a woman with a spear bring Angelica and make her kneel next to me..

A scraggly-haired old woman, face white as bone, and a pale girl, Mary's age, approach the statue with glass jars full of blood—probably from the slaughter. Their clothes are sewn from various-sized patches of dried skin and painted with human figures burning alive. Some of the patches are flattened faces. Who would make a child wear such a thing?

Our captors bow. Part of my mind has disappeared, and I have trouble thinking.

The ancient woman and little girl place their jars in front of the monster, pick up the wooden bowls at its feet, and dump their foul-smelling contents atop the bones spiraling along the tiled floor.

They put back the empty bowls and begin chanting, the old woman's voice harsh and demanding like a crow, the girl's squeaky and darting like a bunting.

> *Who is like unto the beast?*
> *Who can make war with him?*
> *The heavens and angels he smote*
> *The earth and oceans he scorched.*

The little girl pours blood from the jars into the bowls.

> *For the days of wrath are upon us*
> *And who shall be able to stand?*
> *Both awful and beautiful children*
> *Inherit the woeful land.*

The old woman coughs—a deep, bone-wracking noise—then spits bloody mucus onto the floor. She turns to Bone-Beard. "Any others?"

"One girl, young. One boy, infant. Five adults and near-adults slain."

She waves a gnarled finger at me and Angelica. "And these two?"

"Both fertile. The smaller one wants to join. The pregnant one doesn't talk."

"My children," I say. "Where are they?"

The man behind me kicks me hard in the back. Pain wracks my body.

"Rise," the old woman says.

Our captors yank us to our feet.

"Hold them," the old woman says, and draws a dagger.

She approaches Angelica with the knife, smelling like decaying corpses. *Don't hurt her.* But better her than me. Unless I'm next.

But she uses the dagger to slice the cord holding Angelica's eye patch, revealing the empty socket behind. "Recent?"

Angelica hides her eye socket with her arm.

"Open your mouth."

Angelica doesn't respond. Eye-Flames grips her face and pulls her jaw down. She doesn't resist.

The old woman peers inside. "Good teeth." She feels Angelica's bulge and nods. "Healthy baby."

She inspects my teeth next. I take care of them; none are rotting. Then she points her dagger at my tattoos. What if she wants to slice off the skin and add it to her clothes? I try to back away, but Bone-Beard's grip is too strong.

"You have metal birds where you're from?" the old woman asks.

"Only broken ones."

She grunts. "Of course. The world is dead."

I point my jaw at the monstrous statue before us. "What is that?"

"Everything. All that is seen and unseen. All that is outside and inside. All that came before, and all that shall come."

Part of me wants to ask more, but there's no point. "Let us live. My children especially. We're healthy and skilled and can help you."

The old woman points at my left eye. "You should give your friend an eye and she should give you an ear. Or we should offer them to the All"—she gestures toward the statue—"so you match." She nods. "That seems most beautiful."

"What's wrong with you?" comes out of my mouth.

She frowns, then glares at me. "Hold her mouth open," she tells Bone-Beard, "so I can cut out her tongue."

Cut out her tongue. My arms and knees shake. Warm, strong-smelling pee trickles down my thighs and sticks to the inside of my pants. I clamp my teeth together.

Bone-Beard tries to pull my jaw apart, but can't—jaw muscles are incredibly strong. He tries to pry dirty fingers between my teeth.

I give him enough gap to slip in his fingers, then bite down as hard as I can. He screams and I taste blood. Irma would be proud that I'm putting up a fight.

Bone-Beard yanks his bloody fingers out of my mouth.

In my mind, I whirl around and duck beneath my other captor's spear, then twist it out of his hands. I stab Bone-Beard in the chest, right through his armor. He drops to the floor. I swing the spear around and slice the other guard's neck. He grips his throat, trying to hold in the spurting blood. Angelica follows my lead, taking the spear from her female guard and slaying both her captors. I turn again and hurl my spear at the old woman—their matriarch, I assume. It slams into her chest and throws her against the monstrous statue. The statue flies apart and collapses on top of her.

Can I make it happen? I whirl to face the man with the spear. All eyes are on me.

Except Angelica's. She grabs the end of the distracted female guard's spear and thrusts her bulging belly against it. "No pueden tener a mi bebé!" Blood and clear fluid pour from the wound.

My feet seize as if nailed to the floor. The man in front of me jabs me with his spear. Bone-Beard kicks the back of my right knee and throws me to the floor.

Angelica pulls the spear deeper inside, tears dripping from her eyes and mixing with the flow from her wound. The old woman mutters something I can't quite make out, then coughs again.

"Heal her," Bone-Beard tells me.

I'm bleeding from my left breast. The female guard yanks her spear out of Angelica. Blood and baby-sac fluid gush out.

"Show us your healing," Bone-Beard growls at me. "Save her."

Curled in pain, I shake my head. "Not possible." Angelica's baby is almost certainly dead, and Angelica will follow soon. It's better that way. Maybe it's better if I die too, and my children.

No, I don't want to die. And I can't let my children die. Isaac's just a baby. Mary's a darling—smart, loving, sensitive. A better version of me.

I hold out my bound wrists. "I need to use my hands."

The old woman cuts the rope with her knife.

I check my wound first. It's not deep. I just have to wash it out and bind it shut.

I crouch next to Angelica. She's unconscious, her skin white and clammy. I slap her cheek. "Stay awake!"

She doesn't respond.

I pull up her blood-soaked tunic. There's a big gash beneath, just blood streaming out now.

"Can I use your knife?" I ask the old woman. "We have to get the baby out." Angelica's only chance.

She cackles and hands her dagger to Eye-Flames. "You do it."

Eye-Flames slices open Angelica's belly—the blade is sharp—and pulls out a tiny motionless baby, a huge hole in its back. He hands it to the old woman, who shakes it, lifeless arms and legs flopping around and spraying specks of blood.

The little girl—being trained to replace the old woman?—speaks to me. Her childish voice reminds me of Mary, but her face is cold and unsmiling, as if she's never known joy. "You're no healer."

The ancient woman lowers her head toward the child and says, "There's no such thing, High Priestess."

That little girl is this group's leader? I want to shout, 'no healing can bring back the dead,' but I don't want to remind the old woman about cutting out my tongue.

The old woman raises Angelica's dead baby to the statue and chants her crazy words again. She coughs up more red-tinged mucus, then hands the tiny corpse to the child-priestess. The little girl grins for the first time and widens the baby's spear wound with her fingers.

I shut my eyes and hear tearing and chewing. The old woman's crow voice says, "Take that one upstairs. Take the other one to the stockroom."

Someone grabs one of my wrists, grip strong and sweaty, and yanks me to my feet. "Come." I open my eyes. Bone-Beard is holding my wrists and pointing his big knife at me. The other guard pokes me with his spear again, this time not hard enough to penetrate my tunic. They march me to one of the trenches holding train rails. I don't look back to see what's happening to Angelica and her baby—I don't want to know.

We drop into the trench. It smells like old piss, and is full of empty mouse and rat traps. We haul ourselves up to the other side and walk past empty bedding.

Bone-Beard pulls aside a latch and opens a metal door. A terrible smell—shit and piss and rotting meat—enters my nose and I gag. Beyond is a concrete-floored room full of people, maybe a dozen, men and women of varied ages, most of them naked.

I look closer—my mind blocked something. Their legs all end in stumps, some below the knees, some above. Some are missing arms.

I stand there, unable to think. Someone shoves me inside. The door slams shut behind me and I hear the latch slide. There's no light except a faint glow through the narrow crack beneath the door.

I throw myself against the door, but it's solid. I bang the backs of my fists against it. "Let me out! Let me prove I can help you!" I think about my children and scream as loud as I can, "I'll do whatever you want!"

No one responds. Tears run down my cheeks.

I hear noises from further inside. It's too dark to see, but it sounds like the slapping of hands against concrete and stumps dragging behind.

I bang on the door again, as hard as I can. "LET ME OUT!"

The crawling noises draw closer. I turn toward them. Barely visible now in the dim light from the door crack, hunched shadows reach fingers toward me.

"Go back!" I kick at the shadows. My feet connect with hands and faces. I lose both my moccasins.

Something grabs my right ankle and pulls. I lose my balance and fall hard against the concrete. Hands grasp both my legs. My right ankle flares with pain, teeth breaking the skin and tearing at my flesh.

I'm not dying like this. I grab the head chewing my ankle, lift it up, and smash it as hard as I can against the floor. I hear a crunch. Blood and teeth spurt out of the mouth. I do it again, and again, then kick the creature away.

A shadow grabs my left foot and bites down hard. My toes erupt in terrible pain. I feel flesh rip away from the ends.

I kick at the shadow with my aching right foot, then grab it by the hair. I smash its mouth against the concrete, again and again, trying my hardest to knock all its teeth out.

The shadows retreat into the darkness. My toes and ankle are badly mangled and I'm bleeding from three places now.

I don't have a knife to cut strips from my tunic, which is too tough to tear. I spit in my palms—the best I can do for water—and try to wash out my wounds. It isn't enough, so I force out pee on my ankle and toes. I curl against the wall and hold my bleeding feet together. Hannah's curse is complete—I'm paying for our slaughter of the church people. And Angelica's people. Sobs pour from my throat.

Mary, Isaac, I'm so sorry. You should be safe and happy. Without the storm and the following horrors, Angelica would have birthed a healthy baby. A boy or girl who'd be their playmate.

The pain... White flashes pop in my eyes. My feet, such incredible pain. Will the bites get 'fected? What about my babies?

Mary! Isaac! Please be alive!

AFTER A LONG TIME, the door unlatches and opens. The dim light outside now seems as bright as the sun. Teeth are scattered in pools of blood in front of me. The other captives retreat to the far wall. Two drip blood from their mouths. Two down, eleven to go.

Two figures stand in the doorway, a man and a woman, holding spears. One tosses a bloody head into the room. The head of a beautiful young woman with honey-colored skin and braided dark hair. Angelica.

My best friend's head bounces along the floor toward the back. The other prisoners dive for it, mouths gaping.

The door closes, leaving me in darkness again. I hear growls and the tearing of flesh.

The door opens again. I fell asleep! I'm lucky none of those legless beasts attacked.

Guards set down buckets of water. I take one for myself.

They toss in human hands, feet, and bones coated with gristle. The others crawl forward and feed. I hope at least this will keep them from attacking me.

"Let me out!" I insist, knowing it's futile.

They shut the door again and I hear the bolt lock us in.

I wash my wounds from the bucket of water and hope they haven't been 'fected.

Why are they keeping me here? I can help them. I'll do anything not to die. What happened to my children? Are they still alive, or did the creatures out there kill them and eat them? Or will they raise them like the little priestess offering bowls of blood and eating babies? Will my innocent children become insane killers? Which is worse, that or death?

I never should have brought babies into this world.

I LOSE TRACK OF TIME. Then I hear shuffling, the sounds of hands against concrete and dragging of stumps.

"I'm a warrior!" I lie to them. "I spared you before, but from now on, I'll kill anyone who comes close!"

They stop—maybe waiting for me to fall asleep again.

I think about Mary and Isaac and I think about myself and how even an awful life is better than no life at all. Whenever I begin to collapse into sleep, I bite the back of my hand, as hard as it takes to keep awake another few minutes.

THE DOOR OPENS AND several armored men and women enter, some carrying spears, some with clubs. The legless people in the back shout and grunt. They shove and hit each other, each trying to be furthest away. I press against the wall and don't move, hoping our captors will ignore me.

Some of the guards corner two of the legless people in the back and swing clubs against their heads. The prisoners struggle and shriek, but after a few skull cracks, they collapse. The guards haul the limp figures out of the room. It looks like they're both women.

The door slams shut again. Two less enemies to worry about. And now I know what to do next time the guards come—throw others in front.

WATER AND AWFUL-TASTING food that I grab before anyone else. Weeds, dead rats and human remains. I kick and scream at anyone that comes close. I'm weak but they're weaker. Can I kill them all? I'm outnumbered, with no weapons.

I'll rip open their throats with my teeth and drink their blood.

MY CAPTORS TAKE MORE legless creatures, one or two at a time. I make myself hard to catch—scurrying around and pushing others in front.

When it's just me and two others, I pounce on the one that looks weakest. It flails its remaining arm as I pull it into a corner. I smash its head against the concrete until it stops moving. Then I tear at its throat with my teeth until hot, metallic-tasting blood gushes into my mouth. I deepen the wound and drink.

When the flow ends, I start chewing the tender neck flesh.

THE DOOR OPENS AGAIN. I've been here a long time. Bone-beard enters with two other armed men. He points at me and tells them, "The new one."

I stab a finger at the last legless one. "Take that one."

Bone-beard points at the rotting remains of the thing I gorged on. "You're eating our food." The men grab my arms.

"No!" I thrash and snap my teeth.

Bone-beard punches me hard in the stomach and I lose my breath. Another lost battle. I can't beat three strong men with armor and weapons—not even close.

"Let me see my children!" I can't die not knowing if they're alive or not.

Bone-beard doesn't answer. His underlings grip my arms and half-drag me across the train trench and over to the seven-skulled lizard statue.

The child-priestess holds a reddish-tinged dagger. Next to her stands Mary—my Mary! Tears blur my vision. I try to run to her, but my captors hold me tight.

"Mama?" my daughter calls out.

"You alright?" I ask.

"You look awful."

"Where's Isaac?"

"Upstairs. He's fine." Mary grabs the child-priestess's free hand. "This is Karla. She's my friend."

What?

Karla the child-priestess gives a faint smile. "We're the only five-year old girls. Mary's really smart."

Mary grins at me.

Karla says, "My teacher died. We saved you some."

"Some... what?"

Mary brings me a spiral-covered wooden bowl. "I missed you, mama."

Inside the bowl is a bony finger, presumably from the old woman. It's pointing at me.

Are they going to kill me or not?

"Everyone else ate some," Mary says, "This is all that's left."

"I got the tongue," Karla says. "The best soldiers get the brains and hearts, and the priestess gets the tongues."

I hope Bone-beard eats contaminated brains and dies.

"I have your books," Mary says. "Can you teach us to read them?"

I'd forgotten about the plant guide and Bible. What good are they now? Might as well use the paper to start fires.

Karla addresses my captors. "Let Mary-mama complete the ceremony."

They release my arms. I take the bowl from Mary. She's finally found someone her age to play with, but it's with a child monster. I guess the child monster wanted a friend too. Five years keeping Mary alive, now maybe she'll keep me alive.

It hurts my head to think anymore. I'm hungry. I grab the finger and gnaw the dried meat off the bones.

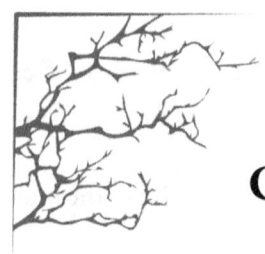

Chapter Ten

Mary
Ten years later

THE FAINT CRYING OF a baby carried over the burbling of the rocky stream. Mary halted and put up a hand. Her two older companions, Von and Karima, stopped and readied their bows.

Von was tall, thin, and dark-skinned. Karima was shorter, with a jagged knife scar running down her cheek. Their torsos were protected by metal plates beneath a camouflage netting of leaves. Instead of hot, bulky armor, Mary wore her mother Lucy's old deerskin clothes, patched and re-patched over the years. This was Mary's fourth trip searching for others, but the first time she'd encountered anyone other than solitary men, too wild and fearful to catch more than a fleeting glimpse of.

"Don't shoot anyone unless they shoot first," Mary told her companions.

"It may be too late then," Von said.

"It is the will of the All," she told them.

Von grimaced. Mary was only 15 and had never fought in battle. But as Under-Priestess, Mary outranked simple soldiers. And Karla, the High Priestess herself, had authorized the reconnaissance mission.

Mary's crazy but knowledgeable mother had advised her to remain friends with Karla and try to fit in. "It's how we stay alive," she'd said. Mary had progressed beyond mere survival, and now helped the High Priestess decide how the community should be run.

Mary and her soldier escorts continued upstream, weaving through gaps in the rhododendron thickets. It was cool enough in the low mountain valley to travel during the day, especially during the winter months. The air was fresh and fragrant compared to the old train station. Too bad her mother and little brother weren't here. Her brother, who was being trained as a guard, had never even seen a forest or stream—at least not since he was old enough to remember things.

The baby stopped crying. Mary rounded a bend in the stream and spotted a mound of leaves a short distance away, half-hidden by shrubs. It was too high and distinct to be natural. She raised her see-far glasses, which had once belonged to her mother's aunt Irma. Mary had only a hazy recollection of her: a mean woman with a sharp voice.

The leaf mound had a triangular entrance. From the darkness within, a woman made shushing noises.

"Stay here and cover me," Mary told her soldiers. She approached the leaf mound and announced, "Hello. I'm unarmed." Not entirely true—she had a bow and hunting knife—but they were secured by straps.

A lean, pale-skinned woman in her mid-twenties scrambled out of the shelter, bow in hand, arrow notched against the string. "Who are you?"

Mary stepped slowly forward, fingers outstretched. "My name's Mary."

"What do you want?"

"I come from the Vanished World city of Atlanta. I'm looking for people like you, to learn what other communities exist."

The woman's eyes widened and she aimed the bow at Mary. "That place is full of insane cannibals."

"Put your bow down," Von warned the woman from one of the rhododendron thickets. "We have a dozen archers aiming at you," he exaggerated.

"Things have changed there," Mary told the woman.

Half the population had died from disease outbreaks, including one that made people shake and twitch and lose the ability to speak. Mary had brought the sick to her mother, who lived in one of the group's other buildings, terrified of everything—especially the train station. She'd been able to treat some of the illnesses, but not the twitching disease, which affected their leading warriors and was always fatal.

"They get it from eating human brains," Lucy told Mary when they were alone.

"They're cooked," Mary objected.

"Cooking doesn't help." Lucy almost never smiled, but this time she did—a wry, secret smile. "Don't tell anyone. They all deserve to die."

Mary had argued with her mother, and decided to announce the disease came from eating human flesh of any kind. The High Priestess had declared an end to cannibalism, and following Mary's advice, the group began raising rabbits and growing crops.

MARY POINTED AT THE leaf-mound entrance. "We can speak inside," she told the pale woman with the bow.

"Just you." The woman crawled back into the shelter.

Von hurried over. "You know what'll happen to us if they kill you. We should light their den on fire and force them out."

"Have faith," Mary said. "I'll shout if I need you."

She entered the dimly-lit shelter, supported by cut branches. It was too low to stand inside. A young dark-skinned man pointed a bow at her. A beige-skinned woman clutched a baby. Woven packs and pouches of supplies were propped against the angled sides, and a book titled *Edible Plants* lay on the grass-strewn floor.

"Cannibalism is no longer practiced in Atlanta," Mary told them. "We only eat rabbits, fish, and plant food now. I'm one of the new leaders."

"Why are you here, then?" the pale-skinned woman asked.

"I'm searching for other groups." The official purpose was reconnaissance and threat assessment, but Mary hoped for more than that. She pointed at the book. "Can you read and write?"

"Yes," the young beige-skinned woman said.

"We have books in Atlanta," Mary said, "in old libraries, printed on special paper." And the plant guide and Bible she'd inherited from her mother, both of which she'd practically memorized. "But I'm one of the only people who can read them." She showed them the *U.S. Army Survival Manual* and *Medicinal Plants of the Southeast* she carried on her expeditions.

"Why are you searching for others?" the pale-skinned woman asked.

"To help them. And thereby help ourselves." She turned to the dark-skinned man. "You can put down the bow. It makes me nervous."

The pale woman met his eyes and waved her fingers downward. He lowered the bow but didn't put it away.

Mary poked her head out of the shelter and told her escorts, "It's safe. We're just going to talk a while."

"I'm Phoebe," the pale woman said. Mary had never met these people before, but the name sounded familiar.

Phoebe pointed at the others. "That's Estrella and Ray. Their baby's named Hope."

"Nice name," Mary said. "Where are you from?"

"Originally south of here, in the flatlands. Our group was a lot bigger then, but we were attacked and driven from our home." Her face tightened. "Most of us were killed or died later."

"I'm sorry to hear that." *Was it our people?*

"We made them pay, though," Phoebe said.

Mary couldn't recall any battles where her adopted people took heavy casualties. They were much better trained and equipped than anyone else they'd come across.

"Phoebe stabbed their two males and started fires in the church," Ray said.

Church? Two... teenage boys?

"Our home that they took," Phoebe added.

"As soon as the rest of their clan arrived," Ray continued, "we trapped them, set the whole forest on fire."

Chills ran through Mary. She was inside a cramped shelter with the last survivors of the church group that her mother's family had massacred. Her mother mentioned the catastrophe often, claiming she'd doomed both groups. Mary couldn't forget the burning church, the screams, Tash and Griff dying, everything ablaze.

Estrella spoke for the first time. "They'll burn for all eternity, Hannah told us."

It took a few moments for Mary to overcome the flood of terrible memories from those times. The deaths and suffering had seared the patterns of her mind, much like her mother when she was a child. *That's over,* she reminded herself. *I have the most powerful order in the region behind me now.*

With clammy hands, she unrolled her map of northern Georgia, copied from an 'atlas' and updated as needed. The atlas as a whole was badly outdated, showing land where now there was water, and farmland that was now expanses of burned pine trees.

"Have you seen any other groups?" she asked them.

"We try to avoid others," Estrella said. After some coaxing, she pointed out the places they'd been, including the church where they'd grown up. The church Mary's family had attacked.

"I advise you not to continue north. The mountains are dangerous." Mary pointed to the top of her map. "Past here, maybe a hundred miles from where we are now, my mother's birth village was massacred by painted-face raiders. She was lucky to escape."

"We're careful."

"You have a loud baby. We found you. The next people will probably not be as nice."

Phoebe stared at the map. Estrella clutched her baby.

"Come back with me," Mary said. "We have security, shelter, and a steady supply of food."

The three church survivors looked at each other.

"And we have a Bible," Mary added. *Their Bible.*

"You're believers?" Estrella asked.

"Yes."

MARY AND HER TWO SOLDIER companions escorted their three recruits—four including the baby—back to Atlanta. They followed the train tracks south and entered a long, cool tunnel. They passed torch-lit underground stations with small garrisons, and finally reached the smoky lower level of the central station.

With the High Priestess's consent, Mary had ordered the stations and tunnels scrubbed clean several years ago to help stop the sickness outbreaks. But the walls were still painted with imagery symbolizing The Fall and the triumph of The Beast. Phoebe, Estrella, and Ray stared at the spirals and wild eyes and screaming mouths, and huddled together, unease on their faces.

Phoebe pointed at one of the screaming faces. "Are these scenes of Gehenna? Hell?"

"More like Revelation," Mary said.

Isaac, Mary's dark-eyed younger brother, ran down the ancient train platform toward her. He was healthy and fit, but still had the face of a child. As a guard-in-training, he carried a bow and spear nearly everywhere.

"You're back!" he said.

Mary hugged him. "Anything happen while I was gone?"

"Same as always."

"I don't suppose mama's here." Mary had signaled her impending return by banging a hammer against one of the train rails, using a code she'd developed. The outposts would have passed her message to the central station.

"You know she won't go near this place," Isaac said.

The answer she'd expected. Mary always felt awkward around her mother, who had taught her many things and loved her children with a fiery intensity, but cringed at the sight of other group members, and often curled in a ball beneath her bedding. She meant well, but had never been strong enough for this world. *A mistake I won't make.* And even though she finally found a stable home for Mary and Isaac, she considered it a failure rather than a success.

Mary turned to the newcomers. "Follow me." She led them past rabbit hutches and empty sleeping mats dotting the long platform.

They reached the wide column supporting the seven-skulled, seven-armed statue of the All. Her mother had thought it a giant lizard because of the coiled tail, but it was actually a wingless dragon, a creature from ancient mythology. Mary heard loud gasps behind her.

Flanked by more guards, Karla was pouring fresh blood into the spiral-covered bowls at the creature's feet. The High Priestess was thinner than Mary, with long dark hair, a pale face and intense eyes. She offered Mary a cup of blood. "Welcome back."

"Thank you." Mary sipped from the cup. The blood was still warm. At least it was from a rabbit rather than a human.

Then she introduced the people she'd brought. They didn't respond, their eyes fixed on the statue and faces scrunched in horror.

"When you said you were believers," Phoebe said in a cracked voice, "are you worshiping *that* thing?"

Karla stared at her. "Thing? You stand before The All. The force that dwells within and beyond us, the force that extinguished the Old World and now guides the Days of Wrath. Without listening to Its guidance, we are lost."

Seeing the looks of shock on the church survivors, Mary felt of flush of embarrassment, mixed with sympathy. Sometimes she forgot how loathsome the statue was. But Karla was right. It more accurately represented the new world than anything her mother, her friend Angelica, or the church people believed. It kept her people unified and strong rather than tearing at each other's throats or succumbing to other groups.

Phoebe backed away. "You... How can you? It looks... it looks like the seven-headed red dragon in the Book of Revelation."

"Yes," Mary confirmed. "The dragon that waged war and was filled with fury." The writings didn't entirely make sense, but nothing from the Vanished World made sense any more. Humanity had opened a door and locked it behind them, and could now only look back through ash-coated windows.

"You worship Satan."

"A word from the Vanished World, where life was different. This is the All. There is nothing else anymore."

"We respect and listen," Karla said.

"We are realists," Mary added, "adapted for the harsh world the Vanished Ones left us. They destroyed Eden, and we were unlucky enough to be born afterward. But we adapt because we must."

She offered the cup of blood to the newcomers. "You can stay here, or in one of the other structures. This land is under our control and you will not be harmed." She owed them that, after the suffering her family had inflicted on them. "We will teach you to adapt."

Did you love *The Survivors*? Then you should read *The Others* by T. C. Weber!

When a corpse with webbed feet and other aquatic adaptations washes ashore during a hurricane, the county medical examiner calls in marine biologist Will Myers for assistance. The deceased's mysterious sister, Andreia, claims the body and asks Will to help figure out how her brother died. Will and Andreia bond over shared tragedies and a yearning to heal a dying ocean as they seek to learn how her brother spent his final days.

Andreia brings Will to her undersea home, part of a hidden civilization inhabited by smugglers, hackers, treasure hunters, and traders—all members of a different species, driven to the edge of extinction by human diseases and climate change. As feelings between the two grow, the investigation into her brother's death leads to a sinister plot by a fanatical cabal. Together, Will and Andreia must find a way to save both humanity and the ocean without imperiling the existence of her species.

Read more at https://www.tcweber.com/.

Also by T. C. Weber

Watch for more at https://www.tcweber.com/.

About the Author

T. C. Weber has pursued writing since childhood, and learned filmmaking and screenwriting in college, along with physics and ecology. His published novels include *Sleep State Interrupt* (the first book of the near-future *War for Reality* cyberpunk trilogy), *The Wrath of Leviathan* (the second book of the trilogy), *Zero-Day Rising* (the trilogy finale), *Born in Salt* (a character-oriented alternate history novel), *The Survivors* (a post-apocalyptic cli-fi horror novella), and *The Council* (a satire of local government and politics). His latest novel is *The Others*, an undersea science fiction action-adventure set off the Florida Keys.

Mr. Weber is a member of Poets & Writers, the Science Fiction & Fantasy Writers Association, the Horror Writers Association, and the Maryland Writers Association. By day,

Mr. Weber works as an ecologist, and has had numerous scientific papers published. He lives in Annapolis, Maryland with his wife Karen. He enjoys traveling, hiking, and diving, and has visited all seven continents.

Read more at https://www.tcweber.com/.